The Bull is not Killed

The Bull is not Killed

Sarah Dearing

Published in 1998 by Stoddart Publishing Co. Limited
34 Lesmill Road, Toronto, Canada M3B 2T6
180 Varick Street, 9th Floor, New York, NY 10014

Distributed in Canada by General Distribution Services Ltd.
325 Humber College Blvd., Toronto, Canada M9W 7C3
Tel. (416) 213-1919   Fax (416) 213-1917
Email customer.service@ccmailgw.genpub.com

For information about U.S. publication and
distribution of Stoddart Books, contact
180 Varick Street, 9th Floor, New York, NY 10014

02 01 00 99 98   2 3 4 5

Canadian Cataloguing in Publication Data

Dearing, Sarah
The Bull Is Not Killed

ISBN 0-7737-3123-7

I. Title

PS8557.E22587B84 1998   C813'.54   C98-931470-7
PR9199.3.D32B84 1998

Jacket Design: Bill Douglas @ The Bang
Jacket Photograph (flower): Tomonori Tanguchi Photonica
Text Design: Kinetics Design & Illustration

Printed in Canada

"The Gypsy Woman and the Cave" from GYPSY FOLKTALES, copyright © 1989 by Diane Tong, reprinted by permission of Harcourt Brace & Company. Quotations from the English translation of Os Lusiads by Luís vas de Camões, copyright © 1952 by William C. Atkinson, reprinted by permission of Penguin Books, London, England. The folk tale "Maria of the Brambles" is paraphrased by the author from an English translation by Michael York. Used by permission of the translator.

We gratefully acknowledge the Canada Council for the Arts and the Ontario Arts Council for their support of our publishing program.

*To Robin Dearing, for strength, wisdom and love.
Thanks also to my entire family and friends,
old and new.*

C O N T E N T S

"If my inspirations
but prove equal to the task,
all men shall know of them."

Luís vaz de Camões,
Os Lusiads

Luís da Silva Jr. Finds a Shoe and Worries about the Future

WHENEVER HE PASSED the Casa dos Ciganos, Luís Dias da Silva Jr. warded off the evil eye with the sign, a splayed-out version of "bullshit" directed at its little door, and in a rhythmical continuation, a flourish really, of the first gesture, he would genuflect for good measure. Padre Perreira was queried several months ago to determine whether this was a form of blasphemy, if perhaps Christ's blessing should be called upon first or even separately, but Luís was merely scolded for believing in spells and curses and dismissed without an ecclesiastic opinion on the matter. It was unusual for the Gypsies to occupy houses, and no one in the village quite knew what was behind the deviation from the natural order, but everyone, including the padre, was wary of its inhabitants. Despite the well-known hazards — the risk of sudden accident or hump-backed firstborn — Luís took the same route to the sea each morning to clear the previous night's effects from his head. "Routines are good," he read somewhere, good for bringing order to all areas of life when the weeds have taken over your garden.

He dove directly into the first impressive swell so the cold water could slap him awake rudely and immediately dissolve the cobwebs around his brain. The regimen served him well as both cure and penance for sins regularly committed. After a vigorous swim, he lay on the sand to allow the residue of hangover to seep from his body, lit the first of several SG cigarettes, and contemplated his failures. He hoped the solitude of morning would infect his mind with silence, wished a magical wind would blow in from Africa to sweep it clear of all doubt and cynicism, but they were stronger than his will, and the winds brought only clouds and rain.

He focused on a grey streak that had materialized in isolation to join sky and sea, creating a single entity that glided with some speed along the southern horizon. February was his favourite month for sea watching, for experiencing the unpredictable elemental treasures blown towards the land mass, and since this had been the worst winter in memory he was fully in awe. Floods were destroying farms in every region of the country, carrying away small livestock and shabby structures, washing away the year's income from crops, and Lisboa was falling in upon herself, sliding down from the heights of the Bairro Alto and Chiado into the narrow gorge, the Baixa, that is her heart. On the beach where he lay, freshly carved boulders of hard sand appeared daily to block the narrow walkways and left crumbling buildings high above, tentatively perched on receded cliffs. In sporadic intervals of geological mystery, the red earth preferred to melt into orange rivers of mud, and a matronly Englishwoman was about to ruin a brand-new pair of pumps as she marched, unknowingly, along the beach. He recognized her Englishness by the particular pinkness of her skin and the walking stick she carried. Only British tourists displayed the peculiar need for walking sticks, and this one would have done well to use hers to probe the mess at her feet.

"Why do they always wear such silly shoes to the beach?" he wondered with contempt. "Are they put on in a moment of whimsy or as an act of pure vanity?" Luís dismissed women's fashion as something to provide a temporary rebirth into someone younger, more sophisticated or alluring, ultimately and inevitably a waste of time, and he noticed it wasn't until this victim sank into the mire up to her ankles that she finally removed the accessories, confirming his belief.

Luís considered telling her the shell beach was farther east, that their location was the junk beach where high tides systematically deposit detritus amongst the rocks, and decided it was not worth the effort of speaking English. Last week he salvaged a psychedelic shirt here, two tennis balls, still with a remainder of bounce, a cane and a set of matching beach towels, one Donny, the other Marie. Today, he found another shoe, the fifth consecutive day, and each time he wondered whose it might be and how it arrived on the shore. This one was brand new, Spanish, and his size — 39. The discovery of women's shoes required no stretch of his imagination: they were likely removed and carried, such as this woman did, heels being a hindrance in the sand at any time of year, and dropped, or left stupidly on the beach as the tide moved in. Sturdy loafers, however fine, would not necessarily come off for a stroll, and men, at any rate, have more sense than to lose such items recklessly.

A single beam of sun broke through the homogeneous mass of cloud to create a diamond patch on the sea, and a solitary fisherman took God's cue. His movement towards the light reminded Luís he had promised his mother a fish for their lunch.

He gathered up his few things to make the short walk to the fishermen's beach. As he rounded the eastern edge of the cliff that separated the two wide stretches of sand, he heard more shouting than usual, grinned, and looked forward to the magnificent boasting he would hear later at the café of the biggest sardine ever caught in the Algarve.

"Eh pa!" one of the pescadores yelled when he came into view. "Go get the G.N.R."

Luís approached the small crowd of men milling about in collective confusion.

"Hurry! Find Montiego. He should be over at Amadeu's and he's smarter than that da Sousa." Smarter was a carefully chosen euphemism for "more trustworthy with such an important find," for the shouting was not over a sardine at all, but a young man's body, fully clothed apart from one shoe that was carried away by a different swell and now rested at the bottom of Luís's gym bag.

He ran as fast as his lungs could manage after half a pack of cigarettes and found Montiego enjoying his customary carafe of vinho tinto to stimulate an appetite for lunch.

"Hurry. A body. On the beach" was all he could manage between great gasps for air.

Montiego didn't like to hurry, liked less for someone to tell him to hurry.

"Catch your breath, Luís," he replied. "Sit for a moment. I'm sure it's not going anywhere."

Luís welcomed the opportunity to rest, and Montiego replenished and offered his glass before taking the carafe to the barman to hold for his return. Luís swallowed half the wine in two needy gulps.

"Now, what's this about a body?"

"It's on the fishermen's beach. Washed up."

"Man? Woman?"

"Man. Come on, we should get back."

Montiego drained the remaining wine in a single swallow, emitted a little burp, and followed Luís out the door.

"Anyone we know?"

"I didn't get a good look, but I don't think so."

"That's something, anyway." Montiego sanctified himself for both the good fortune and the impiety of considering it as such. They covered the remaining distance quickly and in silence.

"Tide's coming in," Montiego observed on their arrival. "Someone help me move him."

The men looked around or slunk away. No one wanted to touch the corpse for fear of the evil eye, and Montiego sighed.

"Is there not a brave son of Lusus present to assist a one-armed patriot? Ai! Who found him?"

"Giuseppe," three said at once, tonally accusing the old man of drawing inconvenience into their lives.

5

"Then you shall help me, Giuseppe. The gods gave him to you, so he is your responsibility." The other men nodded their agreement with the officer's logic while Giuseppe privately cursed the wretched gods.

"Get a net, Luís," he instructed next. "We'll place him on it."

Luís scrounged for the largest in a pile between two beached boats.

"Any one will do," Montiego called out to him patiently. "It doesn't need to fit."

Giuseppe crossed himself before picking up the arms. Montiego did the same at the lighter end, gathered the legs by their pant cuffs to accommodate his single grip, and with a grace of movement out of respect for the dead they gently swung the pale and bloated body onto the makeshift gurney. Once physical contact with death was no longer part of the burden, the body seemed lighter, more manageable certainly for Montiego, and they carried it easily to the top of the beach.

"Anyone know this man?" he asked when the body was safely moved and any lingering traces of misfortune washed from his hand. If he, a member of the Guarda Nacional da Republica for the past ten years, did not know, it was unlikely anyone else would either, but thoroughness was part of his nature now. "Looks like a tourist. Probably took out a boat from the marina at Villamoura and got caught in the storm last night."

Montiego considered the maintenance of a sense of harmony, whether real or imagined, an integral part of his job in the village. He was wishing the sharks had done theirs.

Luís went home without a fish for lunch.

Montiego Commits His
First Mistake

MARTINO DA SOUSA KNEW what to do, having recently completed special training in Lisboa. Although the younger and less experienced of the two officers, he'd been promoted above Montiego as a result of his new understanding, so it was he who typed the report to send to Faro with the body: "Unidentified tourist. Drowned."

"When will they come for it?" Montiego asked him. "It will be smelling soon."

"Tomorrow, the next day. Who knows such things?"

For once, Montiego was thankful for his colleague's indifference to his responsibilities.

"Let's get out of here. I need a drink."

"You are just like an old woman sometimes, Montiego. I don't know why you ever became a policeman."

"Yes, you do. I get seasick."

They were nearly at the café when Montiego stopped suddenly and brought the heel of his hand to his forehead.

"Ai fudis! I forgot to lock the door. Go ahead. I'll meet you at Amadeu's."

Da Sousa found Montiego's need for thoroughness irrational and annoying.

"You think anyone's going in there, knowing there's a corpse in the cell?"

"Humour me my pedantry."

Da Sousa shrugged and waved dismissively, not understanding Montiego's chosen words, but not caring either.

Montiego worked quickly. At the top of the page he wrote the date and a brief description of the man, including his estimated height and weight and a speculation that he was a Spaniard, not merely from the shoe but from his entire wardrobe and the slightly more aquiline features common to that race. He made the prints underneath, then meticulously washed each finger, folded the paper in four and slipped it into his shirt pocket.

Da Sousa was holding court at the front of the café when he arrived, joking with the fishermen about idiotas who don't respect the merciless nature of the sea.

"Likely got seasick and tumbled in while puking over the side. Isn't that correct, Montiego?"

The men laughed in good-humoured mockery, aware that Montiego could get sick on a rough day from the shore if he stared at the rolling surf too long. He had lived with their teasing for forty-five years so played the clown, shared the joke on himself with the men to diffuse their concern over the incident.

Luís sat alone in the far corner, and, after collecting his vinho interruptus, the officer joined him.

"I found one of his shoes," Luís whispered, indicating a brown paper bag on the floor. "I was hoping to find the other one, because they are my size, but I think you might want it as evidence."

Montiego laughed. "Evidence of what? Exceptionally good taste in footwear?"

Luís scowled. "How can you joke? I saw his wrists when you moved him."

"Got caught in a rope trying to save himself, is all."

Luís shook his head and looked away in disgust.

"You leave the police work to the policemen, Luís," Montiego said quietly, calmly, but fixed the youth with a hard stare.

"Ai, da Sousa!" he called out across the room. "Young da Silva here found one of the attractive Spanish shoes. Should we give him the other one to make a pair?"

"As long as he promises not to wear them on a boat and slip into the sea himself."

The men cheered Luís's good fortune and the reiteration of what they could reasonably comprehend.

"There you are, then. Come by the station later today. Now, no more talk of that. Tell me, what is the university boy doing with his life?"

"Wasting it."

Montiego raised a single eyebrow. "I don't believe it."

"Believe it."

"And you are happy about this?"

"No, just paralyzed to do anything."

"No one is paralyzed."

"Are you blind? The entire *country* is paralyzed.

9

Anyone with any sense is leaving." Luís took a long drink of beer. "Surely you've heard the joke. What's the second-largest Portuguese city?"

Montiego nodded sadly.

"Paris!" spat Luís. "It's a national disgrace."

"Things will change."

"When?"

"When you make them."

"Bah! There is nothing for me here. There are no opportunities for educated young men, only for waiters and fishermen."

Most of his friends had fled Albufeira, Portugal or military service and now led what Luís imagined to be bigger lives in Paris, London, Toronto even. Those left behind, for lack of resources or strength of spirit, worked in the bars and restaurants that had been springing up like roadside wildflowers to serve the tourists. Luís considered his own experience as a waiter one of his most humiliating defeats. Crowned with a degree in Portuguese history, he'd expected the great doors to success to swing open for him, to be beckoned into the world of the elites by a smiling face inside. He could, and regularly would, recite with pride the exact dates and destinations of all the Great Discoveries, the heroes involved and myriad goods brought back from every journey. Names, nicknames, follies and accomplishments of each successive king rolled off his tongue in heated debates about the state of republicanism, but to remember whether a table of four ordered bicas or chavenas just five minutes earlier proved beyond his mental capacity: defeated by coffee cups. The grand pinnacle of his success to date was a brief stint as a bank clerk and vague references to promotions for hard-working, educated young men.

"What about teaching?" Montiego suggested. "Premier Caetano has promised — "

"Caetano and his promises! Filho da puta! He is the most paralyzed of all. He wants us to remain a nation of illiterates. We're easier to control that way, aren't we."

"Careful."

"What? You'll arrest me for speaking the truth?"

"Not me, I know you are not a dissident. But others . . . The current situation cannot continue forever. That is all I will say. Hold on."

"To what? If I didn't know you, if you weren't Papa's friend, I'd simply become a thief. I'd rob the tourists, or sell them fake hashish made from pepper and olive oil."

"People do that?"

"Lots of them."

Montiego thought this was quite ingenious and wasn't certain of its illegality. He extracted his tattered little notebook from the pocket of his jacket and jotted down a reminder to look it up.

"You don't want to do that," he said. "What about returning to Lisboa? You could take another position there."

Luís shook his head slowly. "I felt swallowed up there."

In the early evenings, after classes or an unproductive day in the library, Luís would go to the Tejo to sit and breathe. It was one of two places he could relax, the other being the botanical gardens, but with an admission price of 10 escudos he held that location in reserve for extraordinary sessions of moping. Instead, he'd walk down to the Praça do Comércio, to sit in the shadow of a mounted King João I, where little waves gently washed over marble steps to the river, and watched the ferries come and go, the water move serenely to the sea. There was space, nothingness across to the far bank and the outstretched arms of Jesus to comfort him on the hillside. Salazar's monumental bridge, visible as a silhouette against the setting sun, impressed him every time he looked at it, reminded him of the potential for greatness, and in the creeping twilight, he could imagine Camões' nymphs dancing on the surface.

"Faro, then?" continued Montiego.

"Why must I leave my home? Why can't there be something here for me? I like it here."

"Then you'll have to find something to suit Albufeira, create it if necessary."

"It is the government's responsibility to create such things, not mine. If we didn't eliminate the monarchy, they would do it, they'd get back what we once had. Even Spain is considering it."

"Perhaps if people stopped looking back, we'd move forward. Greatness requires the courage of ordinary men. You should know that. Your hero, Henrique el Navigador, never even went to sea. It was his men, his people, who had the courage. He merely had the power to tell them, 'Go, spread the faith and bring me back riches.'"

"Vision."

"Possibly."

"He began it all for lesser men to squander."

At that moment, Luís resented them deeply.

THREE

Luís Sees His First Woman and Is Impressed

HE WAS EARLIER THAN usual for his swim, the beginning of a new and more rigorous routine, sparked, in part, by the incidents of the previous day. The beach was deserted, its smooth and pristine surface marred only by a single set of footprints leading to the sea. Luís calculated the trajectory, accounting for the current, and saw the intruder swimming strongly against the waves. His goal was to reach this man's level of fitness and confidence — to beat the sea — and he felt mildly depressed by the comparison he was compelled to draw. Preferring to swim in solitude, not so much out of embarrassment over his ability as to imagine the ocean was his alone, he sat on the sand to wait.

Like Montiego, Luís was accursed with seasickness, a shameful affliction in a country so steeped in maritime history, so blessed with bountiful waters, and he occasionally thought of moving inland where it wouldn't matter quite so much. But despite his inability to ride on the waves, he loved the sea too much to seriously consider living away from it. The constantly changing colours and rhythms soothed his soul, and the dependability of the tides provided a sense of stability and order in his uncertain universe.

His father had been terrified of the water, and when Luís was just three years old he sent him out in a barco on a hot summer day when the sea was lazy and friendly. Once the boat had travelled twenty feet from shore, he signalled at the fisherman to throw his son overboard to teach the boy to swim. What he would have done had Luís not been able to paddle his way in, he did not consider. Luís arrived safely on the beach, shivering and crying and believing his father wished to drown him for being a naughty boy.

He was trying to recall what he might have done to engender such a terrible notion about his own father when he noticed the swimmer now approached rapidly, sailing on the crest of a perfectly curling wave. Confusion reigned for an instant before reality replaced supposition, a surreal moment for which he was unprepared. He watched as she walked towards him with languor in her stride and nothing but water droplets adorning her skin, sparkling in the early sunlight as the most precious jewels. She moved as though the waves had found their way into her hips, restless with containment within just one body, and he thought she must be a goddess, sent, perhaps, to relieve him of his greatest torment, but knew he had done nothing in his life remotely worthy of such a gift.

"What are you staring at?" she heckled, startling him out of his wonderment. "Have you never seen a naked woman before?"

"Of course," he tried to shout back, but his voice creaked and he was horribly aware that she knew it was untrue. "Just never one quite so beautiful," he added, hoping the flattery would prevent her from deriding him further. She walked directly to where he sat without a hint of shame for her nakedness, causing Luís to feel wholly inconsequential.

"What have you done with my clothes?" she asked, haughty and confident that she intimidated this young man.

"Nothing. I've not seen them."

She swung her long black hair away from her face and drops of water burned his body. A slight shifting of her stance accompanied the movement of her head, and from his position at her feet the pink folds of her pudenda peeked out at him from behind a thin veil of black silk. He closed his eyes. Moments later, mortified by a sudden awareness, he shut his mouth, swallowed hard, and licked some saliva away from its corner.

"Give me your shirt, so I can look for them without you staring at my bottom."

He threw it at her in what he hoped would appear to be an act of indifference. It pleased him that it did little to cover her buttocks, but the feeble attempt at concealment excited him further and he had to roll over to prevent her from observing her effect.

The girl strutted about in a pantomime of searching, though her earlier footsteps still clearly led to the rock on which her clothes lay. When she realized she no longer had an audience, she abandoned the hunt.

"Aha! Here they are," she called out and dressed quickly, though not completely, balling up her skirt to carry instead of pulling it on over her shorts. She returned to where he still lay, curiously uncomfortable, she thought, and handed him his shirt. Luís took it and quickly sat up, placing the garment in his lap.

"Do I get to know who it is who has seen me naked today?"

"Luís da Silva Jr. And you?"

She smiled for the first time, and it was a spectacular rainbow to him, filling her face with a million colours and pulling the sunshine into her eyes.

"Luisa. Pleased to make your acquaintance, Luís. It is a great coincidence, não?"

"I don't believe in coincidence," he replied, trying to sound far more sophisticated than he felt. "Only synchronicity."

She frowned. "Synchronicity? I don't understand your big word."

"Coincidence means a random, happenstance similarity of events occurring without reason, while synchronicity strips away the randomness so that it is meant to be."

"So what is meant to be?"

He threw his hands in the air to emphasize the obvious point of it all. "Meeting one another today. My time on the beach is usually much later, but I'm trying to make a new start today, to force change into my life,

so I came early. Had I not, I never would have met you,
nor had the honour of witnessing your nakedness."

"So?"

"So it is a sign and I must act upon it. To ignore synchronicity is to miss good or important opportunities
in life."

"I still don't understand."

"Have dinner with me tonight. You must. It has
already been determined by fate. Besides, it is St.
Valentine's Day."

Luisa paused as though considering whether to
accept the invitation, but was trying to think of something to say that would not put him off entirely. She
didn't understand what he was talking about, possessed
no cultural reference for St. Valentine's day of love, but
had enjoyed teasing him and experiencing his favourable
reaction to her.

"I never eat in restaurants. I do not trust them to
prepare their food hygienically."

Luís thought this was an odd worry, and wondered if
perhaps she was Jewish, or Muslim, with rules of ortho-
doxy and selection.

"You needn't worry about that," he said. "I know a
very good place."

"Não. It is a rule and rules are important to follow."

"Not if they're not logical."

"Logic has nothing to do with it, Senhor
Synchronicity."

Luís laughed. It was his first real and joyous laugh
in months and the unfamiliar sound of it surprised
him. "Okay, *cocktails*, then."

She tilted her head in the manner of a little bird

wishing to see and he wanted to grab her adorable face, cover it with his hands so it could not mock him with its perfection.

"I'm sorry. It is an English word I am fond of using meaning special drinks."

"That will be better, I think."

"Excellent. Where should I pick you up?"

"I will have to meet you."

"Then it will not be a proper date and your father will not be very impressed with me."

"Please. My father is of no concern to you. Tell me where, or I cannot come."

This disregard for the rituals of courting puzzled Luís, but her mystery and beauty, her most brazen spirit, compelled him to pursue the liaison.

"Do you know Café Latino?"

"I'm not familiar with cafés."

"Rua Latino Cõelho. Near the cemetery."

"I know the cemetery. I'll find it. Ten o'clock?"

He wanted to protest. Why must he wait twelve hours to see her? What trick of God was that? "Perfect," he lied, and as she waved goodbye he felt his tumescence gradually subside and worried that she'd noticed.

FOUR

Luisa Goes on Her First Date

 MINIMAL TRAFFIC TRAVELLED her route at this time of year, mostly carts pulled by lazy donkeys, so she walked in the road, away from the overgrown cacti lining both sides. The prickly limbs would not be cut back until later in the year, when more tourists arrived and their pedestrian presence along the hairpin turns became a hazard.

Three dusty miles lay between the encampment and the beach, and Luisa was in no mood to hurry. Her body was imbued with an unfamiliar heat, a suffusion of new, hotter blood than she previously possessed, and it slowed her pace, made her want to pause and savour the feeling, but reality dictated she use the time to think instead of a believable explanation for her whereabouts that morning and one that could serve her again in the evening. She felt slightly nauseated, with a strange flutter in her belly, and suddenly worried that she was mahrime, polluted by the gadjo. It wasn't an altogether unpleasant sensation, a fact that caused her to speculate it was something different. Her limited understanding was that if she was considered mahrime while menstruating, she would experience cramps and bloating and acne from all causes of pollution.

"So simple," she thought, just as she rounded the last bend in the road. She picked up her pace, excited now to get through the day to reach the evening.

The appearance of her mother standing in the road necessitated a different demeanour. Carminda Barbosa was a formidable woman in size and temperament, the expanse of her back so broad that from behind she would be easily mistaken for a man if the kumpania permitted women to wear trousers. A crooked nose and two missing teeth further attested to her reputation of being a fearsome and powerful bitch. Carminda's legendary evil eye could be cast great distances, when lesser Roma required the object of the curse to be present, and her powers were renowned across Europe, made most famous by an incident in Madrid when she caused Generalissimo Franco's horse to drop dead during an anniversary celebration of his regime's ascension to power.

Luisa had long ago convinced herself this could not possibly be her real mother, that a beautiful and kind woman had been sacrificed for her entrance into the world, and one day her father would reveal the truth to her. Clearly, the sole reason he hadn't done so was to spare her the grief and guilt that would mar her life.

In his absence — arrested and imprisoned six months

ago while attending to business in Lisboa — Carminda had become even more vile, and it was not a rational person who greeted Luisa in the road.

"Where have you been?" she hissed. "I was about to send your brother to find you."

"I'm sorry, Carminda. I started bleeding and had to walk to the village to get some napkins."

Carminda shook her head in an excessively dramatic fashion. "Why can't you just use rags like the rest of us? Your vanity will be your ruin. It will ruin us all. Go and get dressed before I decide to infect your face with sores. We are late and have a long way to go."

Luisa ran to the tent she shared with her mother and sister and changed into the traditional clothes she despised. She quickly braided her hair into two long plaits and attached a sextet of imitation gold coins to the ends. Luisa had real gold for important Roma occasions, but they were not for the market. At the market, an appearance of exotic poverty was desirable so the tourists would not be quite as inclined to haggle over her wares.

Fernando waited impatiently in the driver's seat of the cart and little Carmelita sat in back on a bale of hay that would be the donkey's lunch. She and her sister always dreaded the ride home as, hot and tired, they sat directly on the floor of the cart and bounced for two hours or more.

This month, Luisa was selling rag rugs at the travelling market, pretending to make them herself, though they came directly from China, the labels neatly removed and the ends undone for her to "finish" braiding. Carmelita, dressed in rags herself and instructed not to smile, begged for change, while her brother had the easiest job, wandering through the crowd picking pockets and purses. Carminda Barbosa, playing up her role of matriarch in her husband's absence, supervised her children's earnings between visits and gossip. By the end of the day, she would be passed out in any available shade, under a cart usually, with an empty bottle of aguardente lying beside her. Luisa counted on this and she prayed to Saint Sara to make it possible for her to escape in the evening. She suspected it was not proper to make a prayer asking for her mother to pass out from drink, but surely the patron saint of the Gypsies would understand a young girl's need for a tiny share of happiness.

At the market, people stared at her, some going so far as to take her picture without the courtesy of requesting permission. Occasionally, one of these would flip a coin at her to add to her humiliation. When she was a little girl, she enjoyed the attention and thought the photo seekers viewed her as exceptionally pretty, not as a curiosity to record for friends and relatives back home. She'd smile and wave at the camera and chatter happily, but as she grew older, a sneer replaced the smile in an internationally recognizable look of contempt, and the frequency of the photos diminished. Her mother hoped the lace blouse and brightly embroidered skirt would attract the tourists and their coins, and if she caught her daughter glowering at the world would give her a cuff to the head.

"Pretty girls don't need to use intimidation to get what they want," she had tried to explain to her daughter several years ago. "A smile, preferably a modest one until you are older, will achieve better results."

"You never smile," Luisa replied.

"I am ugly. It is a different life, people expect it of me. But when a beautiful girl displays anything but happiness, people feel cheated."

"Cheated of what?"

"Their own illusions of what will bring happiness."

Luisa brooked frequent, brief visits from young Ciganos, not because she welcomed their awkward attempts at courtship but for the relief of boredom. She had yet to encounter a suitor worthy of an encouraging, coy smile; in fact she practised her contemptuous look on them all prior to investigation. It had become a game, and she awaited a stalwart opponent to challenge her.

The market fostered commerce between the Gypsies, the tourists and the permanent residents, but this safe and legal gathering also allowed the diaspora to maintain communication, exchange important news, socialize and conduct their own affairs without suspicion. It was not uncommon for an entire kumpania from Spain to arrive in Faro on market day, and less frequently, smaller groups from France, Italy, Eastern Europe or Africa. Portuguese officials assumed the Gypsies fixed the schedule for the benefit of the tourists, and never recognized that it ingeniously facilitated their need to have designated meeting times and places.

Negotiations for marriage matches took precedence over the subsidiary business of selling a few cheap items, and the young men were encouraged to use the opportunity to inspect potential wives. Luisa vaguely knew most of the boys present, and was able to quash their amorous intentions easily with a litany of harsh words about their suspected prowess. She wasn't interested in playing the game today, and curtly told all visitors to go away.

The market packed up later than usual to accommodate the last-minute arrival of a tour bus from Portimão, and Luisa considered asking her brother to drop her off on the way home, then remembered her clothes: if Luís knew, he'd never ask her out again, and she had determined she needed to learn about gadje life in order to properly evaluate her own.

"Nando?" she said in the little-girl voice she found to be advantageous with men. "Will you give me a ride to the beach after dinner? I have my bleeding very bad and I want to clean myself properly."

His sister's talk of her filthy state disgusted Fernando, as intended, caused him to feel dirty himself just listening to it.

"How will you get home?"

"I'll walk. The cramps in my belly are terrible and exercise helps."

He weighed the risks and thought of the 300 escudos in his pocket, expropriated from his takings before relinquishing them to his mother. It would be wise to spend the coins quickly on a little recreation of his own, and if Carminda awoke to find him gone his sister could be blamed.

"Okay, but you will have to answer to Mama if she ever wakes up."

Luisa rolled her eyes and nodded compliance.

They dragged her to her tent then, muttering and flailing, and deposited her on the straw mattress.

Carmelita was fed some beans and slabs of thick fried bread smeared with fig jam, and placed in the bed beside her mother.

Luisa quickly slipped into a simple cotton gingham dress that was several years old, given to her by her father for when they were needing to blend in in Lisboa, and the bodice could now barely contain her newly developed breasts. She undid the top buttons for comfort, and the effect, unknown to her in the absence of a mirror, was that she'd burst forth at the slightest movement. To hide her disobedience, she covered her legs with a long skirt and pulled on a sweater.

Once Fernando had disappeared in the shadows of the dark and narrow street, Luisa removed the outer clothing and hid the little bundle under a sprawling cactus. At the market, she had stolen a pair of white shoes with high heels identical to those she saw the tourist women wearing. They were too small, and she found it difficult to walk on the cobbled street. The tiny metal tips of the heels wobbled on the uneven surface and occasionally stuck in the cracks between the two-inch stones.

Luís was already seated when she arrived and she waved to attract his attention away from the view of the moonlit sea. The dress elicited the desired response, for he stood clumsily to greet her, bumping the table and slopping his drink.

"How is it possible that you are even more beautiful than when I saw you this morning?" He didn't know where these words came from, and as soon as they spilled from his annoyingly dry mouth he felt silly for them. "But you are. Here. This is for you."

He passed her a bunch of young rosemary sprigs tied together with a piece of red ribbon from his mother's sewing box.

Luisa instinctively drew the bouquet across her nose and inhaled delicately. "What is it?"

"*Ros marinus*, meaning the spray of the sea in Latin, which is exactly how you appeared to me today. It is rosemary, the herb sacred to remembrance and therefore to friendship."

"Thank you. I am sorry to be late for the beginning of a friendship, but my brother was particularly slow in his own preparations for a secret night out."

Luís's smile faded. "But why must it be secret?"

"Our mother is strict about whom we see."

"Why? Who does she want you to see?"

"I cannot tell you."

"Of course you can. You just won't. Where does she think you are?"

"Swimming."

"In that dress?"

She pouted and thought she might have to resort to tears. It seemed unfair of him to force her to lie when she simply wanted to experience how the rest of the world lived.

"I put it on only for you."

Her bottom lip looked so delicious, as plump and bitable as a ripe fig, that Luís felt as though he would die of hunger if she denied him a taste.

"I'm sorry," he said. "I'm being rude and didn't mean anything by it. You are a mystery and it is confusing to me. What would you like to drink? Café? Cerveja? Vinho?"

"What are you drinking?"

"Whiskey, but it is not exactly a drink for young ladies."

"Vinho, then, branco, with some ice."

"Certainly. Perhaps you'd like some mineral water in it. It's an American drink, I believe, called a spritzer."

"Spritzer," she tried. "Yes, I like that."

Luís went to the bar. While he waited he could not resist turning around to assess his good fortune. The barman was an enterprising young American for whom Luís and his crowd feigned admiration in order to spend their idle time listening to his imported music on the bar's record player. He proudly pointed out his date, and Luisa provoked a low whistle and conspiratorial wink, causing Luís to suddenly panic.

"What is she doing with me?" he wondered. He'd never had success with females, owing primarily to his inability to talk to them, and the few dates he had been on passed in uncomfortable silence until such time as the lateness of the hour permitted a polite suggestion of going home. He looked around the room to check out the competition and observed no one but safe couples scattered about the room.

"Spritzer for the lady," he announced, handing her the drink.

She sipped tentatively at the straw. "Mmm. Very refreshing. Where did you learn of this American drink?"

"The tourists at the disco. The women drink them so they won't get drunk and act foolish. They don't realize they appear foolish no matter what they do."

"How are they foolish?" Luisa could not believe the wealthy, sophisticated women she had encountered were fools. She envied them, hated them, but admired them nonetheless.

Luís thought for a moment. "They wear too much make-up, for one thing, and clothes that do not suit their shape simply because they are in fashion. Sometimes, for fun, I tell them my name is Vasco da Gama or Fernão de Magalhães, to hear their reaction. They never tell me it is a great coincidence to have the name of a brave explorer."

Luisa gave a little laugh to mask her own ignorance of such grand names.

"What do you do with your days, when you are not at the beach or mocking tourists?" she said.

Luís considered whether a lie would elevate his position in her eyes, but could not think of one quickly enough. "I look for work, read, listen to music here and talk to friends about opportunities abroad."

"Do you wish to go somewhere?"

"No, but I am ashamed of my country for what it has become."

"And you think another place will be better?"

"I know people living in Canada who make so much money, they are able to live well and send money back here to their families."

"What do they work at there that you cannot do in Portugal?"

"Construction, mostly."

"But there is building all over the Algarve."

"Yes, but here it is forced labour for Africans. It's not only the money," he continued, passion taking control of his voice. "A person cannot speak his mind without getting himself thrown in jail. Take the three Marias, for example, charged last month with writing pornography because they dared to question the role of the family in society."

Luisa nodded as though she concurred with his outrage. "What would you do, if you had the choice?"

"Promise me you will not laugh?"

"I promise."

"I would write adventure stories about brave Portuguese explorers, like cowboy western novels, but on the seas. The world has forgotten about us and our accomplishments. I would remind them through my stories."

"And what prevents you from doing so?"

Luís sighed. "It is madness to consider being a writer in a country controlled by censorship. It is impossible to find motivation, inspiration."

"My father always says success at anything is only one part inspiration and nine parts perspiration." As soon as she spoke the words, she wanted to bring them back into her mouth. They revealed too much and caused Luís to scowl.

"My father believed that too and worked himself to death."

"I'm sorry."

"Sim," he agreed.

"Please excuse me. Where is the W.C. Senhoras?"

"Just past the bar, to the left."

He watched her and breathed deeply to calm his nerves, turned his attention to the music broadcast throughout the bar. Luís learned much of his English from listening to lyrics, easy phrases of American notions of romance he hoped would hold him in good stead one day: "let's get it on," "hey, baby, take a walk on the wild side," and his as yet untested favourite, "sexy motherfucker." He recognized the song now playing from the winners of that year's Eurovision music competition, and listened intently.

"Why is a Swedish group singing about someone named Fernando?" he wondered. He preferred either more bitter or sexy music, and since records were scarce and expensive, most frequently obtained by friends returning from trips abroad, he could not afford the luxury of his own collection. He considered what music Luisa might be interested in hearing, and thought of Barry White, even though he became mildly envious when he listened to the man, so obviously experienced in all acts of sex. He returned to the bar and asked if it might be played, appropriately on Valentine's Day, and was given assurances that it would be played after the American's selection.

"You'll like this next one, some cat from New Jersey who really rocks."

Luisa had needed to escape the conversation and wanted to confirm she did not look foolish in her old, childish dress. She had no concept of the allure of the contradiction that stared at her from the mirror, only that her breasts were sufficiently exposed in the fashion of the foreigners. No, she did not look foolish, she decided.

The W.C. Senhoras was spacious and luxurious and she explored all its parts, memorized every detail to reflect upon when back in the encampment and using fig leaves instead of soft tissue. A number of features perplexed her (how the water from the tap was made hot, where the toilet emptied) but these, she sensed, she should know about, so selected what seemed to be the least obvious for explanation.

"Why do they put two toilets in the little private room?" she asked when she sat down again. "It seems to defeat the purpose of the walls."

Luís laughed. "One is a bidet, not a toilet. For washing after."

"Oh," she said, blushing. "I've never seen such things."

"Not at all. It was Salazar's obsession with hygiene. Every public establishment must have them, I suppose, just in case he visited. It is an irony when so few of us have our own toilets."

"It is a good idea, I think. Tell me, if it's so fancy in a regular café, what is it like at the disco?"

"You've never been?"

Luisa shook her head and smiled sheepishly.

"We shall go tonight, then," said Luís.

"I can only stay out for an hour or so."

Luís frowned and examined her for the first time with a critical eye.

"You are only fourteen or fifteen years old, I think. I was fooled on the beach because you have the body of a woman, but you are just a child, really."

"I am not a child," she replied defensively. "If I have the body of a woman, and all its functions, that I am fifteen is of no consequence."

Luís shook his head. "If I am caught with you naked on the beach again, it will be of grave consequence."

"Then I will wear a silly bathing costume, if that will please you."

It did not. Luís had visions of many future blissfully naked mornings together, in fact he had thought of nothing else all day, requiring a trinity of masturbatory sessions.

"Finish your drink," he said unpleasantly. "I'll take you home."

Luisa was angry now. If she was old enough among her own people to marry, why was it not good enough for the gadjo?

"I think you are the one who is the child. If you could see your face. You look just like a little boy who has had a piece of candy taken away from him."

"That's how I feel. I thought, after your performance on the beach, tonight would turn out differently."

"How?" she challenged. She knew exactly what he had hoped for, but wished to tease him and punish him for ruining the night.

"Never mind. It no longer matters."

"Of course it matters. Perhaps I can make it up to you."

"You cannot suddenly become older than you are."

"Não, but I can prove to you it does not matter. We can still begin a friendship. Please. I don't have any friends and am enjoying the new experience. Meet me tomorrow at the beach. Same time."

"I'll think about it."

She kissed him on both cheeks the way she'd seen it done and left him to brood over several more glasses of whiskey.

Senhora da Silva Entertains for the First Time Since Her Husband's Death

 OF COURSE HE WENT to meet her, earlier than the previous day even. He sat on the rock where her clothes had lain and pivoted his head from left to right in all too frequent intervals while he chain-smoked. He stared out to sea in case she came to him from its depths once again, a mermaid; explication of her mysterious ways.

Thousands of years of pounding surf had created a cave in the far side of the western cliff, and he'd brought a blanket to place on the cool dirt floor inside. He'd be the one to look the fool if he had misinterpreted, but Luís considered the assurance of her comfort on this potentially crucial day worth the risk to his machismo.

Like his hero Henrique, virginity taunted Luís, and while he tried to find a little solace in the exalted company, he mostly felt like an abject loser for it, unseemly and perverse. Sexual experience topped his list of missing accomplishments to remedy, and he hoped Luisa would lead him through that particular door.

The beauties of the beach provided insufficient distraction from anxiety over his impending performance, so he searched for an exceptionally interesting shell to present to her. As each was discarded as unworthy, he switched his quest to a fan of coral that he might use to tickle her skin in a tentatively flirtatious gesture of his intent. When tidal water reached the pillar of sand on the beach, he ruefully accepted she was not coming, gathered up his loathsome blanket and went home without a swim.

Each day for the remainder of the week, he set up vigil in the same spot, willing her return. The ocean now repelled him, for he thought of it caressing her naked body: a pleasure denied him, and he was jealous of the sea. Instead, he swam illegally in a succession of new apartment-block pools, claiming to be Mark Spitz when confronted by bored security guards. The rosemary bushes along his route became the object of his increasing bitterness, and he would rip off branches from the most carefully pruned hedges, torment himself with their fragrance before casting them to the ground.

Senhora da Silva fretted over her son's increasing despondency and surliness, and the soiled sheets she now changed each day. A child's sexuality is a difficult concept for a mother to face, and she prayed to the Sovereign Queen to make it be a good and virginal girl virtuously tormenting her son. If her husband were alive, he could talk to the boy, reassure him and discover what the problem was, but the only male she could think of for the job was the policeman Montiego, so she paid him a visit at the station.

"I often think of you, Montiego, without a wife to cook for you, and would be honoured if you would dine with Luís and me this evening."

Montiego had also noticed the change in the boy's mood and associated it with the discovery of the body and their conversation that day.

"It will be *my* honour, Senhora, and I will bring the vinho."

"He requires a man's ear, I think."

"Then I'll bring them also."

Luís da Silva Sr. died one Sunday morning while preparing for church. His wife found him sitting on the toilet with an expression he might wear during a particularly satisfying bowel movement, and this look of pleasure caused Odette to speculate on the involvement of angels in his passing, but made it difficult for her to immediately understand that he had died.

They had not prepared for death, had bought no plot, so she'd been forced to rent one of the little chambers stacked like safety deposit boxes along the cemetery walls. She visited number 169 each Sunday after church, and though she had placed a large vase of red plastic carnations behind the little glass door, the corners of the casket were not quite concealed and it disturbed her, caused her to worry that her husband's soul could not be at peace if his remains were so nearly exposed to the physical world and its inhabitants.

Luís suggested selling the house to acquire enough money to bury the man properly, but Odette convinced her son the correct solution lay elsewhere. It was his house now, to keep or dispose of, as Portuguese law favours the descendants of its deceased over their wives. Senhora da Silva had faith that her son's character and intelligence would enable him to make something of his life, at which time they could rectify the atrocity.

If he ever stopped moping. She went to his room to wake him from his siesta, entered without knocking or even considering such. A well-thumbed magazine lay open on the bed, providing Senhora da Silva with an unwelcome glimpse of pendulous breasts, and Luís lying naked beside it, his erect penis pointing directly at her.

"Ai!" she wailed at the sight of it and covered her eyes with her hand. "Put that thing away." Always a practical woman, Senhora da Silva swallowed her disgust at her son's sinful behaviour. "Get dressed and go pick some caldo from the field by the cemetery. Montiego's coming for dinner and I'm making soup." The words of everyday normality helped to compose her, and she turned her back.

Luís reached for the little pile of clothes on the floor by his bed. His underpants were not among them, used earlier to catch his gism, then thrown across the room in a spurt of self-loathing, so he dressed without them.

"I hate going by the cemetery. Doesn't it grow somewhere else?"

"I'm sure it does, but I don't know of it. It wouldn't hurt you to visit your father now and then. It might do you good, in fact."

"It fills me with shame."

The statement outraged Senhora da Silva and she swung around to face her son.

36

"Don't talk to me about shame as you lay there naked with that evilness in your hand. The only shame you are entitled to is that you are squandering all that he did for you."

Luís did not need to be told this. Without a further word to his mother, he stomped out of the house, ineffectually without the weight of shoes to make noise.

He knew caldo grew in the garden behind the Casa dos Ciganos, and a mere hop over the crumbling stone wall stood between him and his quest. The act of petty thievery gave him a small thrill, so he grabbed a lemon from a tree. He took a circuitous route home, pausing along the clifftop promenade to suck on the sour fruit and rub its oil in his hair while he scanned the beach below for a familiar body.

Obsession had pulled him into its paralyzing vortex. Though he told himself he was searching for one of his remaining friends, the churning of his stomach belied the rationalization. It wasn't simply the dashed hope of experiencing his first real taste of a woman that caused his depression: he had constructed Luisa into his personal saviour — something to lift him out of his boredom, to live and work for, and he fantasized about her constantly. He imagined raping her that night she disappointed him, taking her for his very own forever. After he had run the scenario to a satisfying conclusion, he performed a hundred Hail Marys and repented further by imagining sheltering her like a fragile flower, honouring her tender body with gentle kisses.

Montiego sat reading a newspaper in the front room, a bottle of vinho before him, and Luís was momentarily confused by another man's presence in his house, seated in what he still considered his father's chair by the fire.

"It's good to see a young man returning from a little honest hunting and gathering," said Montiego, looking at the large bunch of caldo in Luís's hand.

The use of the word "honest" disturbed Luís and made him nervous. Could it be possible he had been seen? Had someone called the police not only to arrest him but to mock him as well?

"I'll just give this to Mama and be right back."

The soup stock of chicken broth and potato boiled furiously on the stove in keeping with the general atmosphere of the kitchen. Senhora da Silva took the greens from her son with uncharacteristic impatience, chopped off the stems in a single swipe and began to shred the large leaves into thin strips.

"He has been here a half hour already. I cannot entertain our guest and cook dinner at the same time."

"I'm sorry. I was speaking to Papa and lost track of the time."

The lie pleased his mother and she put aside the knife, ceased her martyring.

"Go and have some vinho with him before dinner."

Luís chose a Sagres from the icebox instead and reluctantly joined Montiego.

"I have missed your conversation down at Amadeu's, Luís. I see you briefly and then you disappear. Where have you been keeping yourself?"

"Here and there. I've been spending a lot of time at the beach thinking."

"Too much of that can be dangerous."

"I don't consider thought to be a negative pursuit."

"Of course not. It all depends on where the mind takes us, though, doesn't it."

Luís looked around the room as though searching for an item to pick out for discussion.

"Take me, for example," Montiego continued. "If I thought of certain things, I fear I'd go mad."

"What things?" Luís asked, not really interested, but eager to keep the conversation away from himself as subject. His eyes flicked to Montiego's loose sleeve, unpinned and obscenely vacant.

"Not that. That I always think about. It is what keeps me sane, believe it or not." He rubbed the stump affectionately. "It is my touchstone, a reminder of what is truly important." He paused, considering what that might be for Luís, and took a long pull on his wine. "Some of us know from a young age the direction our lives will take, and we follow along a singular path to reach a goal, maintaining a steady course until we die. It is not necessarily without obstacles or minor bends along the way, but without major deviation from the initial objective. Such has been my pathetic little life: a straight line. The other, and I imagine fuller, type occurs as a square room. The person stands in the middle with doors all around him. He keeps opening and entering those doors until he finds one that suits him, or he may spend his entire life opening and closing doors. It is more difficult, but I think I would have preferred it."

"When did you decide you wanted to be an officer?"

"I never did. I detest it to this day."

"What did you want?"

"It was never an option — what I wanted. Want is a word of luxury for me, and what I do not think of."

"I find that very sad."

"Don't. You can't always get what you want, but with faith, you get what you need."

Luís grinned. "That sounds familiar."

"Rolling Stones. They are not so original. I've known it for many years."

"What if they are the same thing: want and need?"

"Ah. They seldom are. That is where most people get into trouble, mistaking one for the other."

"I think I want someone to just push me through one of those doors."

"So join the army if you want someone else to run your life. They're desperate for young men to go and get maimed in Africa."

Luís did not respond. He felt ashamed that he had avoided the army as a student and now, as the only male in the family, while Montiego sat before him with his empty sleeve, his sacrifice to colonialism.

"This dictatorship has survived for forty-eight years because of that attitude. You are a man now, Luís. You must begin to act like one. We all must."

"I want to. I don't know how."

"I think you may have the two backwards."

"Should I live like Papa, and die of exhaustion before I reach fifty?"

"Your father had no regrets."

"And I don't want any either about slaving away my entire life while a select few get rich."

"You are smart, Luís, but you don't have many options right now. Take a position, make some money, and save. Then you will have something to use to begin your own endeavours. Who knows what this country will look like five years from now. The opportunities might be falling from the lemon trees."

"So they should." Luís took a long drink from his cerveja. "Tell me, Montiego, who was the man on the beach?"

Montiego considered the character of the youth before responding, tried to assess whether the information would be beneficial, and decided the ignorance and apathy among this youthful generation wearied him sufficiently to risk passing on his dangerous speculation.

"In my opinion, and you cannot repeat it to anyone, he was a Spaniard, an organizer for the communists who are terrorizing that country. They are all around us, trying to join forces, to convince us they hold the answers to our troubles."

"Do they?"

"We would simply exchange one set of fanatics for another."

"Who, then?"

"If I knew, I would be among them now, and convincing you to get off your ass and join us instead of having this current conversation."

Luisa's Nightmare

 WHEN LUISA RETURNED from her tryst, Carminda sat waiting at the entrance to their tent, working on a fresh bottle of aguardente. Fernando squealed eagerly in the face of his mother's wrath, hoping to curry favour and deflect queries about his own whereabouts that evening.

"What lies will you create for me tonight?" she snarled at Luisa. "You are nothing but a spider spinning a web of lies, but now you are caught in it."

"I am tired of lying," she replied defiantly. "I only wish to have the life of a normal girl. I am tired of being treated like a prisoner."

Carminda lurched up from her stool and with her forward momentum increased by alcoholic insanity, slapped her daughter on both sides of the face.

"A prisoner? That is what you think? I will show you what being a prisoner is."

She grabbed Luisa by the arm and pulled her roughly through the compound, past the men sitting around the fire talking and playing guitars. Their dark eyes flashed at Luisa as she passed, making her afraid and embarrassed. Carminda tied her to a tree and spat in her face before leaving her to consider her behaviour.

The rosemary tickled her skin where it lay tucked between her breasts, and when she bent her head she could catch its fragrance, soothing her. She knew it was wrong to say the things she did, to show her lack of respect and to be with Luís and wondered if she really was evil and in need of cleansing. The other Ciganas her age didn't act this way and they stayed away from her, sensing, perhaps, that she was bad.

Once, during a wedding preparation in which all the Ciganinhas participated, she experienced something approaching friendship with the others, but ruined the moment by asking the bride-to-be what it was like to be in love. The poor girl burst into tears and demanded she leave before she jinxed the marriage, shouting the worst possible curse at her: "May your name be forgotten." Luisa did not understand what taboo she had committed and felt for the first time that perhaps she did not belong.

She spent the entire next day and night without food or water or the opportunity to relieve herself in a sanitary way. Strains of music, of spoons and voices and the newly arrived Hungarian's violin, filtered into her consciousness. Snatches of lyrics of a familiar song about hate were grabbed out of the air and made her own as she sang along, hoping to draw strength from the words, but they only caused fresh tears. She tried to fit new lyrics to the music, but happiness didn't match the melody, regardless of her attempts, and she gave herself up to it. Carminda came on the second morning wielding the large knife used for skinning animals.

"Are you ready to apologize?" she asked, waving the weapon in the air. "Are you sorry for treating me like a dog?"

"I have done nothing wrong," she said obstinately. "Go ahead and kill me. I'd prefer to die."

Her mother used the blade to hack off Luisa's beautiful hair, leaving only great ugly tufts about her head.

"Perhaps this will cure you of your superiority."

When Carminda left, Luisa cried. She did not make a sound, but the tears coursed down her face. She cried steadily for two hours and then, like the turning of a tap, she stopped. All her shame, self-pity and hatred had flowed out of her. She felt calm and strong and ready to get herself out of this mess, without stubborn pride as an obstacle.

When her mother came again that evening, Luisa turned the tap back on.

"There is something wrong with me for the way I have been behaving. I am sorry and will always treat you with the respect you deserve from this day on."

Carminda cut the ropes.

"You are not going to risk the honour of this family. I don't know who you have been meeting secretly, but now he will not want you. Go wash yourself. You stink like a gadjo."

SEVEN

A Donkey Sanctuary Is Foiled

 MARGARET BROWN STOOD, hands on hips, surveying her property with smug satisfaction. The villa was taking its intended shape: a pseudo-Moorish structure with rounded walls and plenty of those charming chimneys that dominate the rooftop views in the region. An overgrown vineyard sprawled lazily across one acre, picturesque in its uncultivated state, brown and knobby and reminiscent of her husband's knees.

She was pleased with herself on a number of accounts, not the least of which being she'd bought the five-acre property for a mere 5,000 pounds sterling. In less than four months since taking possession of the abandoned farm, she had also rescued a donkey and nag bound for the slaughterhouse, two wandering, half-starved dogs and a litter of kittens found in the trash bin at the end of her road. Her dream was unfolding as she'd envisioned from the day she set foot in the Algarve two years earlier.

She and her husband, referred to exclusively as Darling whether she meant it or not, arrived for their annual fortnight vacation and, during the hot, dusty drive from the airport in Faro to their holiday apartment, watched an old man shoot his ass in the head for refusing to pull its load any farther in the stifling heat. The taxi driver laughed at her when she requested he stop to assist the dead animal. Her Darling scolded her with sarcasm.

"What do you want to do? Bury it?" he asked, and she knew she was being illogical.

The vision remained at the forefront of her mind throughout the trip, compounded by the recurrent fracas caused by stray dogs roaming the beach, the streets, swarming the main square in packs as large as a dozen. A family of seven cats lived harmoniously on the balcony of the vacant apartment below their own and they invaded her deck each morning when she ate her boiled egg and toast soldiers in the sunshine. Finally, a trip to the butcher to procure bones for the dogs led to the sighting of a further unfortunate donkey being led around to the back of the shop.

That evening, over a poor meal she could barely touch for fear the meat was the same beast, she announced to her husband the idea she'd been ruminating on all day.

"Darling, when it is time for you to retire, I'd like to settle here in Albufeira and open a refuge for all the abused and abandoned creatures. Just think how far your pension will go in a country as poor as this one."

Darling murmured an unenthusiastic "Yes, dear"

and poked suspiciously at his own dinner. He thought his wife a bit of a fool and had no desire to live out his retirement without running water, reliable telephone service or a decent plate of haddock and chips.

The poor old sod didn't live out the year, though, succumbing to heart disease after sixty-two years of grease and an affection for the local boozer. His insurance company paid out on his life and Margaret inherited the pension from the bank where he'd spent his life. She sold their modest bungalow in the village of Rye, arranged for the eventual removal of her belongings and set off to fulfil the dream she believed Darling had shared.

It was all so simple. The property was advertised in the *Anglo-Portuguese News* and its owner was in a great hurry to leave the country as a result of some unspecified difficulties with the government. Margaret Brown considered politics a distasteful interest for a proper woman, and the problems of her resident country and its citizens were no exception. Slightly intimidated by the urgency of the owner, and thinking her brief prenuptial employment as a legal secretary ample training, she signed the agreement and paid her money without the benefit of counsel.

Although she suspected them of fecklessness and inclined to be lazy, the workers building her house were strong and willing to accept the small wage she offered, provided it was cash. Because they took two hours for lunch, a southern custom not in keeping with her English sensibilities, she made them work until the sun went down, holding a thick bundle of escudo notes in her pocketbook as motivation for their cooperation. The men were paid nightly in this fashion, hats in hand, humbly accepting the meagre fruits of their labours. She was growing impatient with them because the weather had prevented acceptable progress, and while a stone house already stood on the property it had no running water or power, and required extensive repairs to its roof and walls. Her intention was to convert it to a kennel once her initiative was fully under way.

The English contractor originally estimated a three-month job, which didn't take into account the daily rain. Four had passed and the consensus was that another two would suffice, weather permitting. Margaret drove to the site twice a day now, to feed the animals and to ensure the men were at work and not sleeping in the shade of the broad-leafed fig trees.

Her vigil over for the day, she was about to return to her apartment when two ancient cars rattled up the long driveway.

"Who could that be?" she said aloud. This invasion called for a repositioning of hands on hips, an authoritative stance Darling had adopted during their arguments, and one that she had always found expressive but rarely daunting.

A middle-aged Portuguese woman heaved herself out of the front passenger seat, followed by a young man of about twenty and finally the driver, reluctant and shifty and somewhere in the indeterminate thirties. The second, slightly newer and cleaner vehicle contained a single fifty-something smartly dressed man.

"Boa tarde, Senhora! Is your husband at home?" The man knew no husband existed, he was testing her, seeking a reaction that might indicate what degree of challenge lay ahead.

"My husband is deceased. Margaret Brown's the name." She extended her hand but the man ignored it in a deliberate display of chauvinism that had the desired effect.

"Vasco Consuela. I am the advocate for these people and they tell me you are trespassing on their property."

"Their property? I bought this property six months ago. I have the documents at my residence. They must be mistaken, confused."

Senhor Consuela translated into Portuguese, and the woman waved her arms and spoke rapidly, pointing and scowling at Margaret Brown.

"Excuse me. She asks from whom did you buy the land."

"Carlos Pacheco. I paid him a great deal of money."

At the sound of this name, the woman began to shout and wail. The driver shouted. Only the younger man remained calm and, thought Margaret Brown, looked about with the air of a simpleton.

"I'm afraid there is a misunderstanding, Senhora. Carlos Pacheco had no right to sell this property. It belongs equally to him and his seven brothers and sisters. The permission of all must be given in writing and I do not believe that occurred."

"Surely that is not my problem, but the rest of the family's."

Senhor Consuela tried to look sympathetic. "You are wrong, Senhora. You must stop building until the matter is investigated and resolved."

"This is a trick, isn't it? One of those third world shim-shams. How much more do they want?"

"It is not a matter of money," he replied, his tone

indicating great offence at the suggestion. "These people are in disagreement over whether to sell the land at all. Four others are out of the country and must be contacted for their opinion. And then there is the matter of finding Carlos, to hear his side of the story."

"But he is in Germany. He told me had a position as a matador in Munich."

The lawyer suppressed a laugh, nodded sagely and lifted his palms in a gesture of helplessness.

"Well then, it's a matter for the police," Margaret Brown announced. "Please, how do I contact you?"

Vasco Consuela fished in his shirt pocket and pulled out a tatty business card not at all consistent with his appearance. Margaret Brown took the card, glanced at it, and with a little puff of indignation walked to her car.

Once she had disappeared in a cloud of dust, Manuel Pacheco strutted to where the workers stood around and shook hands with João Gueterres, his informant.

The men knew from the outset their employer had no right to the land. Upon being approached with the opportunity for work, João went straight to Manuel.

"A foreigner believes she has bought your place up on the hill," he said. "Someone has tricked you and she now wishes to build a villa."

Manuel instantly recognized this as Carlos's scheme, for he'd suddenly disappeared without a word about his destination.

"We need the work, Manuel, and after everything is built, the Englishwoman will have to go home and leave the pretty new villa for you."

"Or she'll pay more than the land is worth to avoid the trouble," he responded.

So they all waited until it was too late for the foreigner to give up easily.

Manny saw this as his big opportunity and secretly thanked his younger brother for taking action with the useless farm. He staged his announcement to his mother and half-witted brother Paulo, crying that he intended to work the old quinta that season.

"I went out to draft a plan for where to put the favas, to examine the state of the vines," he lied. "I went to sit in our old house and dream of the possibilities. My heart nearly stopped when I saw what was happening. I am getting my shotgun."

Senhora Pacheco raged at the injustice, but urged her son to contact her brother, the lawyer from Faro.

"I do not trust lawyers as much as my shotgun to settle such matters," Manny replied.

Senhora Pacheco pleaded. "You are too honourable to risk going to jail for shooting an Englishwoman."

"An Englishwoman! You are right. If it was a Portuguese man, I'd have no option but to protect my property with whatever means. Her foreignness complicates it, though."

EIGHT

Luís and Paulo Visit the Ciganos

HE WANTED A DENIM jacket, a gift to himself to lift his spirits, so when the notices for the market went up around the village, Luís invited his friend Paulo to get a ride on his motorbike. Paulo admired Luís as older and educated, and occasionally Luís took advantage of his esteem. He had been good friends with Paulo's older brother Carlos before he mysteriously disappeared six months ago, and it was his motorbike Paulo inherited, for which he gave thanks nightly and slipped in a little prayer at the end that his brother would not return to reclaim it.

It wasn't far to walk, but much more impressive to arrive with noise and speed. The Gypsy market provided the youth in the Algarve with a selection of fashions otherwise inaccessible to them. Either the local shops were too expensive or their goods too Portuguese, meaning not American-looking. A young man wishing to distinguish himself from the fishermen and farmers, without spending a month's wages, relied on the Gypsies to bring him style: flared trousers, wide lapels, and Lewis jeans and jackets so close to the original, an untrained eye was often fooled into thinking they were a bargain. Luís very carefully cut the authentic red tabs off drunken tourists at the disco with an X-Acto blade and sold them for a few escudos or a glass of whiskey for future transplanting on the imitations.

Caravans formed haphazard aisles to display merchandise in an approximation of a store, but without the luxury of order or logic in the placement of goods. Brightly painted pottery was sold off the same table as laundry soap and cassette tapes of three-year-old rock and soul from America or England. Cheap platform shoes were brought from the north, made by children paid a few escudos for their labour, their little fingers most efficient for the jobs of lacing and gluing of various adornments.

As Luís surveyed the stalls for the best prices, Paulo followed, eating wads of hot deep-fried dough dipped in sugar. He ate three, the size of an Englishman's hand, during their meandering.

Luisa saw them through a billowing curtain of lace tablecloths. She had anticipated this placement of Luís in her path so had come prepared. Around her head she'd wrapped a large scarf to hide the shame of her hair and the yellowing bruises in the shape of Carminda's fat fingers. She drew it closely to her face so that it resembled a hood, and leaned forward to scrutinize some imaginary detail in the rug on her lap.

She felt rather than saw him pass, and did not dare look up for fear that he'd experienced a similar sensation of collision without contact.

"He cannot know. He cannot know. He cannot know." She repeated the mantra silently one hundred times before she allowed herself to raise her head and look about. He was gone from view, but Luisa kept a watchful vigil for his return.

Luís found a selection of affordable jackets and he preened excessively in black versus blue, his torso assessed in a hand mirror held at a distance by an eager Cigano. Paulo wandered off to more interesting displays of merchandise: transistor radios, football decals and iron-on patches, key chains of a naughty nature. He was trying on a pair of aviator-style sunglasses when he heard the shrill voice of Margaret Brown. Peering around the corner of a caravan, he spied her, one palm outstretched, haranguing a Gypsy woman.

"I gave you 1,000 scudos." She thought a moment for the correct word. "Mil scudos." The Cigana shook her head and Margaret Brown nodded her own in a single abrupt retort.

"Quinhentos," the Gypsy said politely and proffered the 500 note in her hand.

"A simple parlour magician's trick," said Margaret and looked about for help. "Hello!" she called out, seeing Paulo, waving frantically in his direction, but he ducked quickly out of view. "Bloody hell!" she cursed and turned back to her transaction.

A young man, rousted by his mother for assistance with the dispute, tried out his fiercest look on the woman before him.

"You go," he snarled, pointing.

"I'm getting the police."

"Go!"

She turned, frightened suddenly, and as she moved away the Cigana rubbed the 500 bill that had indeed been given to her and threw the bad energy back in Margaret Brown's direction, causing a slight shiver to run through the recipient.

As Paulo wound his way back to where Luís was waiting, he was distracted by a black puppy tied to a table. The moment he reached down to touch its tiny head, a small boy was at his side announcing, "Purebred Labrador, only 500 escudos." Incredulous that anyone would part with such a treasure, Paulo pulled out the last of his savings and pressed the note quickly into the boy's hand before he changed his mind.

"Where the hell have you been?" said Luís when his friend reappeared. "I was about to leave."

"I saw someone I know and then I bought this little dog. Isn't he beautiful? I named him Cãozinho."

"You can't just call a puppy Puppy."

"Why not?"

"It's dumb."

"But I'd call him that anyway, whatever his name was, so it's really smart."

Luís thought to argue, then thought not. There was a certain logic somewhere in his friend's reasoning.

"Come on, let's go. You want me to hold him while you drive? Or maybe I can drive."

Paulo didn't know which to give up. He thought Cãozinho might be placed inside his jacket while he drove, and he picked him up to test his idea. His jacket was too tight and the puppy too squirmy, so he told Luís he could drive.

At the exit from the market, an old woman sat in their path, dressed in heavy black garments despite the warmth of the day. What set her apart from the thousands of Portuguese women like her was the teen-aged girl sitting on her knee, slumped inwards to reveal a bare back, grotesquely humped. A sloppy sign pronounced three more at home to feed, and a dishbin beside it held small offerings to their plight.

Paulo deposited the last few coins from his pockets into the bin.

"Don't be such a goddamn idiota," said Luís.

"Am not an idiota. Take it back."

"That's the oldest trick in the book and you fell for it. That makes you an idiota."

"They're desperate."

"They're crooks. Shameless, dirty thieves. Wait here and when everyone is gone, the girl will get up, put on a proper shirt and help her grandmother or auntie, or whoever the hell she might be, collect their takings and go."

"But they still must be desperate to do that."

"Not desperate. It's instinct. They've been doing the same thing in varying degrees for five hundred years. It's in their genes, like animals."

Paulo stroked the small head of Cãozinho.

"I know you been to university, Luís, but I don't believe you."

"Then don't. Be an idiota, but take a look at that dog's tail, how it curves. Look at its feet and I'll bet they're webbed with six toes."

"So?" said Paulo, confirming the extra digits on the oversized paws.

"So it's nothing more than a mongrel, part Labrador, but mostly Portuguese water dog. Wait and see, its legs will never grow in proportion to its body and it will be just like any dog you could get for free anywhere. You've been tricked, my friend."

"I don't care. I like him."

Luís rolled his eyes. Parked next to where they left the motorbike, a Cigano sat in an ice-cream truck cheaply converted from a regular van, smoking and scrutinizing the crowd.

"Let's get an ice," said Paulo.

"Do you have any money left?"

He realized he hadn't, shook his head, and kicked at some dirt.

"I'll treat you to one since you drove," said Luís, feeling slightly guilty for reproaching his friend earlier.

Paulo perked up immediately, his embarrassment abandoned easily. They approached the truck and asked for two Olá Calliopes.

"I don't have any. I'm only selling the van. You want the van? Only 10,000 escudos, but just today."

"Hey, Luís," said Paulo, "why don't you buy it? You could sell ices to the tourists this summer and make a whole lot of money."

"I have no desire to spend my time selling ices," Luís snapped. "But it is a fine vehicle and I could convert it into a caravan, maybe, or use it to make deliveries." He wondered where he could quickly get the cash.

"I'll be back in an hour," he told the man. "Don't go anywhere."

NINE

Montiego Speaks of the
Tragedy of Pedro and Inês

MARGARET BROWN DROVE directly to the G.N.R.
station from the Gypsy market, directly, that
is, after passing the tiny, nondescript building
twice and being forced both times to drive up the
narrow and steeply winding street because of honking
cars behind her. Annoyed, frustrated and equally weary
of both twisting the stiff steering wheel and concen-
trating on not stalling the old Citroën, she finally just
parked in the valley and walked the few blocks.

Montiego sat at a small metal desk and had just
unfolded a copy of *Republica* to look, not so much for
news, but for obvious omissions and lies dictated by the
censorship commission, a surrealist parlour game he
called Truth or Scare.

"Meu Deus," he shouted just as Margaret Brown
strode in, startling her and causing her to assume that

the comment was directed at her.

"I don't speak Portuguese," she said curtly. "I hope you speak English because I am at my absolute wits' end."

Montiego looked up from the newspaper and irritation settled into the deep lines of his face. The biggest news in forty years lay before him and he was obligated to deal with a tourist with a stolen pocketbook. He briefly considered asking her to wait, glanced back at his newspaper to confirm it was real, and breathed in patience.

"A very little English," he replied, forcing his mouth into his best policeman's smile. "What troubles you? Slowly, please."

"I was just now taken for 500 scudos at the market. And threatened," she added for weight. "But mostly I am here because I bought land and am building a villa and now these charlatans say I do not own the property because the man did not have the permission of his entire family."

"Merda," Montiego said involuntarily, his smile disappearing over the inconvenience of such a time-consuming complaint. "The man's name, please?"

"Carlos Pacheco."

Montiego whistled. "Manny Pacheco come see you?"

"I don't know. There seemed to be an entire family, with a solicitor. My house will be complete in two months. The situation is ridiculous." She stiffened her lip to stop its trembling.

Montiego shook his head. "It is the law, I fear. I can ask Carlos to return your money, but . . ." He shrugged a little to not raise any false hope.

"He said he was going to Germany, to be a bull-fighter."

Montiego threw up his hand, still an effective and recognizable gesture of futility in its singularity.

"And what, may I ask, does that mean?"

"It is the same in English, I believe," he said.

"How dare you be so dismissive. Is this how you treat all foreigners?"

"Please. Sit. I did not mean to dismiss your problem. You are tricked. There are no bullfights in Germany."

Margaret Brown sat rigidly, composed and righteous to mask her embarrassment, in the chair across from Montiego.

"They are a treacherous familia. I will tell you a story if you have moments."

Margaret Brown sighed and nodded her agreement. "Only a few moments."

With his limited English, Montiego related the well-known tale of Pedro and Inês.

Inês de Castro was born of a distinguished Castilian noble family and came to Portugal in the entourage of Constanca, the wife of the Infante Dom Pedro. She and Pedro, the heir to the throne, soon fell passionately in love. This did not suit the monarch, King Afonso IV, who feared Spanish dominance and sent Inês back to Spain. Pedro had to accept his father's decision, but did not forget the woman he loved. When his wife died giving birth to a son, he had Inês brought back to Portugal. He lived with her quite openly and the couple had four children.

The king still worried the Spanish de Castros would become too influential and had the Privy Council order the death of Inês. She was murdered in Coimbra in the Jardim das Lagrimas, the Garden of Tears, as it henceforth was known. Pedro dreamt of revenge but was obligated to bow to his father's will. When King Afonso died in 1357 and Pedro succeeded to the throne, he ordered those who had taken part in the murder of his beloved to be most cruelly tortured and executed. Only two of the three killers were found and he ripped their hearts from their bodies, one from the chest and the other from the back. Not entirely satisfied, he exhumed the corpse of Inês and crowned her queen in a macabre ceremony in Coimbra Cathedral. When he died, they were buried foot to foot so that the first thing he might see, come the Resurrection, was the face of his beloved.

The third killer was never found. Assisted by a beggar, he hid in the stony villages of Beira. Families bearing his name, Diogo Lopes Pacheco, are numerous there, and every June, those who claim descendancy celebrate his escape with a picnic and endless jugs of wine.

"What, may I ask, is the relevance of this fable?" asked Margaret Brown.

"It is no fable, Senhora, it has been repeated in more than two hundred works of literature, including Camões' famous *Os Lusiads*. I am telling you it is bred in them to be treacherous."

"That is of no help to me."

"It is always of help to know with what you deal, não? I will speak myself with Manny. Where do you stay at?"

Margaret Brown wrote her name and temporary address on a slip of paper and handed it to Montiego.

"Margaret Brown. I am Rui Montiego." He extended his hand as he rose to indicate the interview was concluded. Margaret Brown shook it without enthusiasm.

"You can tell Mr. Pacheco that I too will be contacting

a solicitor. I will be in touch with the British consul also. It is an atrocity."

"Pois, pois," replied Montiego, using the polite Portuguese interjection of mild interest. "I will be touching you."

Margaret Brown looked askance at the man before her.

"Bloody hell you will," she replied before realizing this was only a lapse of language skill. "You will be in touch," she corrected, and left.

Montiego did not register her reproach, as he had already returned to his paper and its astonishing news of the publication of a book by General António de Spínola. *Portugal e o Futuro* boldly called for the end to thirteen years of war in the Portuguese colonies of Guinea-Bissau, Mozambique and Angola, and postulated that they were unwinnable by military means. This national hero, the former governor general of Guinea-Bissau, dared to proclaim that the war effort had prevented Portugal from catching up with the development of its European neighbours. The newspaper contained incendiary passages that Montiego read in a combined state of euphoria, disbelief and fear.

"Today Portugal is living one of the gravest hours, perhaps the gravest hour, of its history."

He looked up from these words to consider this cheeky move by the general and noticed for the first time a large black stain of mould on the wall spread out in the shape of a rooster. He hoped it meant good fortune, for such blatant criticism of the government would level the label of dissident on Spínola's head, and would surely mean exile. He glanced at his watch and decided to see Manuel Pacheco on his way home in an hour's time and settled back to his newspaper to search for Premier Caetano's possible reasons for allowing this bomb to be dropped.

His reading was once again interrupted, by a breathless Luís this time.

"What is it, Luís? What has happened now?"

"Nothing has happened. I need 10,000 escudos. You are the only person I know of who might have it."

"What makes you think I have 10,000 escudos?"

"You work."

"What do you need so much money for?"

"There's a van for sale. I wish to buy it and use it to make some cash. You'll get your money back, I am certain, and if not, you may have the van."

"What would I do with a van? I couldn't afford to put petrol in it."

"Please, Montiego. I swear, I will even use it to cart tourists to the airport in order to pay you back. It is a great opportunity to do something, like you told me."

"I see." Montiego laughed. "You think because I told you to create an opportunity, I am also somehow responsible for assisting you."

"Not responsible, exactly. Come on. We can be business partners if you wish."

Montiego considered his small bank balance and thought of the new sports jacket he'd intended to spend it on.

"Okay. In the name of Portugal's future, I will assist you, but if I catch you squandering this opportunity, I shall have the right to discipline you however I see fit."

"It's a deal. I promise, there will be no need for discipline. Shall we shake on it?"

T E N

Pequita Annabela

 LITTLE ANNABELA GONZALEZ WAS found under a
hibiscus bush not far from her home. She
could have been sleeping, her angelic face
peaceful, framed by cascading ringlets and several
large crimson flowers fallen by her head.

Word spread quickly, but not to the police. Da Sousa
could not be trusted and Montiego was considered
impotent under his thumb. At ten o'clock, more than
fifty men packed into the restaurant that served as this
month's discreet designated meeting place.

Senhor Felipe Gonzalez chaired the meeting, it being
his daughter.

"Muito obrigado to all of you for coming here tonight,"
he began. "I think you've all heard of the terrible crime
committed, the rape and murder of my beautiful pequita
Annabela."

There was a loud murmuring amongst the men.

"The filho da puta who did this must be caught, or it will be one of your sweet daughters next. The police in our village are influenced by politics and no longer care about justice. It is left to us and I ask for your assistance."

The crowd gave their agreement in varying degrees of enthusiasm, some extreme, others more tentative.

"I don't believe a Portuguese is evil enough to commit such a barbaric act. We are all good Catholics. Therefore, it must be an outsider. We are plagued by an encampment of dirty Gypsies not three miles from here. Any one of them might have done this and I propose we go there this night and get one to show them all this is a village to fear and avoid in the future."

Their anger and frustration, cumulated over so many years, was released as a single roar of agreement.

"Go home and get your shotguns and we'll meet at midnight at the entrance to the cemetery."

Martino da Sousa
Gets Some New Pets

 SINCE HIS RETURN from the capital, Martino da Sousa felt like a new man, invigorated and reinvented as a powerful captain of the campaign against subversion. His wife, Maria, saw only a strange evilness that had apparently taken control of her husband, a vile and inexplicably pathetic beast contained within his skin. Never romantic in nature, da Sousa now refused to look at her during their sex acts, entering her instead from behind and, on some occasions, violating her in a most painful and humiliating way. She dreaded the night and began to postpone bedtime with unnecessary chores to avoid his touch, but he was insatiable and she would be awakened by his rough hands groping under the sheet. After the first such time, she went to church to pray for her husband's soul and confessed her participation in the filthy act. She sought the advice of Padre Perreira, told him she felt sick in her heart, and was confused by his instructions to seek out her own salvation through a pilgrimage to the shrine at Fátima. She could find no fault of her own, and committed a grave sin by questioning the judgement of the holy fathers, so she outright refused to allow her husband to defile her body and accepted his rage as a preferable alternative.

His meanness was not confined to the bedroom: da Sousa unleashed a violent temper on her when she denied or simply displeased him. He had a legal right, but she wished whatever diabo possessed him would move on.

For several weeks, da Sousa had been adding to the flock of pigeons kept behind their house high on the hill overlooking the village. Each evening he brought another home in a bit of abandoned fishing net, caught in the square in the centre of town where they gathered for pieces of bread distributed by an otherwise unoccupied soul. Once the coop was crammed with a solid mass of birds, the smell of guano unbearable in the entire yard, da Sousa released them all and shot the birds out of the sky, one by one with his service revolver as they came home to roost.

Maria witnessed this act, wailed for the Sovereign Queen to hear, gathered a few possessions in a cardboard box and fled to her sister's house.

It was inconvenient of his wife to leave him, but not worrisome to da Sousa, for he knew she would return after a few days of whingeing and complaining. He quite enjoyed the peace of a solitary house, with no one to swipe his feet off the table or sigh at having to pick up after him, and simply took his spare uniform to his eighty-year-old mother to wash and iron.

The Policia Internacional e de Defesa do Estado, or Directorate-General of Security as it was officially renamed in an effort to distemper the past, recruited da Sousa one evening at the disco where he was unsuccess-fully trying to seduce a group of Swedish schoolgirls. The deal presented to him consisted of three weeks of special instruction at their training centre in return for a raise and promotion. His report on the drowning victim amounted to the first act of fascist-style censor-ship of events he'd been able, in his new capacity, to commit, and it gave him a sense of finally having done something of importance. He was bored with the petty infractions and complaints of a sleepy village: disputes over trespassing goats and borrowed tools, unlicensed cigarette lighters and children playing football in the streets.

He and Montiego were not friends, never had been, owing to differing philosophies on life and their chosen roles, so it surprised da Sousa to see Montiego, out of uniform, walking up the laneway to his house on a Sunday morning.

"Eh pa!" called da Sousa amicably.

"Olá. Bom dia. I am sorry to bother you on the Holy Day, da Sousa, and your day off, but there is a crisis which requires your authority."

On his walk to work that morning, Montiego had cut through the square to ensure no sleeping drunks were present to offend the tourists when they arrived for their white coffees and cups of tea. There, slowly turning in the fresh breeze, a short Cigano hung from one of the jacaranda trees, a dozen dogs sniffing and barking at his boots.

"Jesus!" shouted Montiego. "What the hell is going on?"

He wasn't equipped to remove the body himself, and couldn't just leave him swinging there, for the square would wake up in an hour. He ran to the fishermen's beach to solicit assistance, but it was oddly deserted, even for a Sunday morning, the red, blue and green boats still lined up on the shore. He scanned the beach and saw a lone figure sitting in the sand.

Luís responded casually to Montiego who was waving his one arm and shouting at him. He got up and approached without haste.

"Have you been in the square?" Montiego asked him. "Não."

"A man has been hanged. A Cigano. Jesus. This isn't P.I.D.E. They do not hang and they aren't interested in the Gypsies right now."

"How do you know?"

"I work with one of the bastards. I know da Sousa and his style. You must help me remove him before the tourists arrive."

"Perhaps they need to see him, for a little excitement to take home with them."

Luís's attitude bewildered Montiego. "Do you know something about this?"

"Maybe our special policeman is bored with drowning and shooting his victims. This is far more dramatic."

Montiego knew da Sousa had a touch of madness these days, but was still sceptical of his involvement.

"It cannot get into the international papers. I will lose my job. There will be hell to pay for everyone."

Montiego cut the rope while Luís held the small man.

"He stinks. Ai! He shit himself!" Luís spat the bile from his mouth.

Da Sousa was amused by Montiego's news. "It's a shame they didn't just torch the encampment, got rid of the lot all at once."

"It is still a crime, da Sousa, regardless of what you think of the victim."

"Não, my friend, you are mistaken. It is community service."

"So you are not going to investigate?"

"I will question the villagers, though I'm certain they will not know anything. I am very curious, however, as to why they did it."

TWELVE

God Is a Spaniard

"PORTUGAL IS REALLY NOTHING more than a poorer part of Spain," declared Margaret Brown as she reached for her third custard tart. "Perhaps if the Spanish had held on to it, it would not have these insane laws allowing people to get away with fraud." She bit vigorously into the pastry, causing it to collapse, and the warm creamy filling oozed over her fingers and chin.

Her companion for afternoon tea, Harry Young, was a retired solicitor who had opened Sir Harry's English Pub in the square the previous year and now spent his golden years listening to such tirades from fellow ex-pats and lonely tourists. He had secretly hoped to receive the distinction of knighthood upon his retirement, for thirty-five years of dedicated service to the Empire, and when he did not he left England in a huff and put the title in front of his name himself. The running of a pub was easy work, and he quite enjoyed his new role as confidant and adviser.

He discreetly passed a napkin and practised a look of compassion on Margaret Brown.

"What's wrong? You appear puzzled," she said.

"No, no," he said and pointed to his own chin.

Margaret dabbed daintily at hers before continuing. "The G.N.R. officer, Monty something or other, was kind enough, but seemed more interested in telling me some outlandish folktale relating to the family name. Very unprofessional, actually."

"These are difficult times in this country. Montiego's mind may be elsewhere."

Margaret sighed heavily, took a sip of her tea for its constant comfort.

"Have I made an awful mistake? Is that what you are trying to tell me? That I'm a fool?"

Harry reached across the table and patted her hand.

"Wait for Jorge Rego's opinion. I know too little about the law here." He did consider her foolish, had nearly wet himself laughing when she told him her predicament, for who in their right mind would consider buying property from a man claiming to be a bullfighter, in a foreign country and without counsel? She was the most self-centred, silly woman he'd ever met, and he encountered them daily in the familiar milieu of his pub.

Harry also met the twenty-five-year-old lawyer in his bar one night during a lull in tourist traffic. His family was responsible for building many of the finer hotels in the Algarve, the prodigal son acting as legal counsel for the operations, and that evening, Jorge bemoaned the lack of interesting legal challenges in his life. When Margaret Brown contacted Harry to seek his advice, he immediately contacted the young man.

As he glided across the terrace, women and men alike stopped conversations or attention to food to stare and to see who would be blessed with his deiform presence. His grace and obvious ease within his own aurous skin was enviable and intimidating, particularly to the more austere, pallid British tourists who sat in the sun with handkerchiefs covering their balding heads. With a bundle of crisp U.S. dollars in his pocket and the latest glitter fashions draped over his mannequin form, he amused himself with middle-aged women desperate for a final shot at romance and, as such, willing to do just about anything he requested. He carefully selected those he could easily dispose of, ascertaining in advance that they would depart in a week or less. Hearts were broken and packed off home with each weekly planeload of faded English roses.

"My apologies for keeping you waiting," he said. "I had to see a friend off at the airport and traffic was kept to a mule's pace by a funeral caravan of Gypsies."

"De nada," said Harry, always eager to show off his small collection of Portuguese phrases. "Good to see you again. This is Mrs. Brown. Margaret, Jorge Rego."

Margaret held out her hand and it was kissed, rather than shaken, which embarrassed her slightly.

"Thank you for joining us," she said.

"My pleasure, Senhora. It saddens me that one of my countrymen has acted with such dishonour against a fine Englishwoman. I admire the English very much, having had the good fortune to attend school there in my youth."

The retirees exchanged glances over this placement of youth in the past tense.

"I have filled Mr. Rego in on the details, my dear. Where would you like to start?"

"I need to know my options."

"A court proceeding will take a long time, even if it is possible to find Carlos Pacheco, which is very unlikely. There are houses everywhere sitting empty, in states of semi-completion, for exactly the same reasons. I'm afraid it is a common trick. Your best option is to pay off the remaining family members."

Margaret Brown shut her eyes for a few moments while she considered this. "Make it all just go away," she wished before opening them again.

"I am not a rich widow, as these people obviously believe."

"Richness is relative, Senhora. Please, try to understand, these people have nothing."

Margaret Brown was incapable of understanding.

"The only matter of concern to me right now is that I too do not end up with nothing. One person's wealth over another's is irrelevant. Is it not?"

Rego nodded sagely.

With her eyebrows knit, lower lip extended to create an expression most unseemly on a grown woman, she exclaimed the only truth she really knew. "It's unfair."

"We have an expression in Portugal for when events out of our control seem to seek us out personally to destroy our good fortune. It is that God is a Spaniard."

"If God is a Spaniard, the devil himself must be Portuguese."

Rego laughed. "We are not all bad. I propose I contact the family's solicitor and try to get a sense of what they are after. Has Rui Montiego spoken to you since you made your report?"

"Not a word."

"He is a good man. His hands are tied in the matter." He smiled smugly. "An unfortunate choice of phrase, I fear. Leave the matter with me. I will speak with him also."

Margaret nodded half-heartedly.

"I suggest you consult your financial adviser and determine exactly how much more money you are prepared to spend on the property. I'm sad to say that this is the way of my country these days."

Rego departed with the same suave movements, as though his entrance were simply played in reverse for those who had missed it. The English couple watched his exit in silence and Harry removed his golfing hat, thinking a little colour on his face might be attractive. Margaret grabbed the remaining tart and slumped back in her chair.

"What am I going to do?"

"Pay them. They won't ask for much."

"Why is everyone trying trying to cheat me? I was even cheated by a Gypsy the other day over these sandals." She raised her foot to display a crudely made mule with cork platform soles.

Harry grimaced. "Don't go to that place, dear. They're all rogues and will put a curse on you just for the fun of it."

"Surely you don't believe in curses, an educated man like yourself?"

"One cannot be too careful."

"Put your hat on. The sun is getting to your senses."

"I'm glad you're able to maintain your humour. I know it must be difficult. Why don't you come round to the pub for supper this evening and I'll fix you some nice grilled sardines and baked beans from home. I might even open a can of mushy peas for you."

She smiled thinly. "A bit of home would be lovely. Now I think I'll take a good long walk to clear my head."

They parted company with awkward, unpractised cheek kisses and Margaret descended the rough steps to the beach. The final drop was greater than the others, the sand eroded by high seas and rain, and in her agitated, distracted state, she fell off her shoe, went over on her ankle hard enough to tear the ligaments. The cheap leather band of her sandal came unglued with the twist and she dropped to her knees.

She sat on the sand, covered her face with sticky hands and sobbed — not from the pain, but the frustration and humiliation of it all. After a few moments, she recovered her decorum, removed the other shoe and threw the pair with all her force towards the sea. They landed pathetically close to her and she looked away in disgust, took a deep breath and called out shakily for assistance.

THIRTEEN

Rego Shows His True Colours

BENFICA WERE PERFORMING shamefully, so all at Amadeu's were in foul humour when Jorge Rego entered in search of Montiego. His appearance elicited suspicious stares, for this was a working man's café, a refuge from all manner of unpleasantness: rain, heat, women and children, tourists of course. Interlopers were made to feel so unwelcome they quickly left and suspicions were particularly high on football days, for any stranger could easily be a Sporting supporter, in enemy territory to stir up a challenge.

Montiego sat with Luís, watching the match with superficial attention. Spínola's book occupied his thoughts — for the most part, where he could get his hands on a copy.

"Boa tarde, Montiego," said Rego, slapping the officer's back in a gesture of friendship he did not truly feel.

"Jorge Rego! What the hell are you doing in here?"

"Looking for the finest G.N.R. officer in the Algarve."

Montiego shook his head at the obvious lie. "Sit! This is Luís da Silva Jr. He too is one of our proud educated sons."

The younger men nodded acknowledgement at one another and made their mental assessments. Luís disliked Rego's looks and apparent success, and Jorge dismissed Luís as a peasant.

"What can I do for you, Rego?" asked Montiego.

"I come on the matter of Margaret Brown and Carlos Pacheco."

"You know Carlos?" Luís asked.

"Não, the charlatan is not known to me," Rego replied. "A Senhora Brown has engaged me to resolve a dispute involving Carlos Pacheco and his family. He is a friend of yours?"

"Yes, although I haven't seen him in several months. He seems to have disappeared."

"Precisely, and he did so with quite a large amount of my client's money, paid to him in good faith for a property he had no right to sell. Montiego here was going to speak to his brother."

"Paulo?" asked Luís, incredulous.

Rego sniggered. "If only it were. No, the crafty one, Manuel."

"I spoke to Manny," said Montiego. "They want more money."

"I know they want more money. They are like

Ciganos, those people. The question is, how much? She claims not to be wealthy."

"Manny didn't go into specifics with me."

"I have convinced the woman the matter is best resolved outside of the courts, and she is anxious to continue the work on her villa, which, I hear, is incredibly ugly and a poor attempt to mimic our fine Moorish styles. Have you seen it?"

"Não."

"Are you attempting to find Carlos?"

"I have sent a letter to the German authorities, as she claims that is where he is, but I do not hold much faith in the information."

"She is a stupid woman, without question. However, she has been swindled and deserves the chance to salvage some of her investment. Besides which, she is threatening to contact the British consulate, and that could put a political twist on the matter that would be harmful for everyone."

"What more would you like me to do?" Montiego asked.

"I'd like you to determine how much Manuel wants so we can be prepared with our own offer. You might be able to make him understand the Senhora acted in good faith in the matter, that it is not her fault but his brother's."

"I don't know, Rego. That doesn't sound like the way I conduct my business."

Rego's pleasant facade evaporated and he glared across the table. "So I've heard. There are certain interests which require more protection than others. It is perhaps a lesson you need to learn."

"Are you threatening me?"

"Not at all. I am informing you of the current reality. Your general is incapable of changing that."

Montiego kept his rage from surfacing to deny this prick the satisfaction of a reaction.

"I am not in the habit of manipulating the people of this village," he said. "If that is what you desire, I suggest we turn the case over to my associate, Martino da Sousa. Perhaps it is the best solution for all concerned. In fact, consider it done. I will have him contact you immediately. Now, if that is all, please leave us to the football match. We have already missed two goals."

Rego was gliding out of the café when Benfica scored its first goal, and was knocked off balance by a patron jumping to his feet.

"You stupid oaf," he said, wiping at beer splashed on his jacket. "Watch what you're doing."

"What did you call me?"

Rego realized his error. "Nothing. I'm leaving."

He didn't have time to dodge the man's fist and went sprawling into the crowd at the bar, knocking more copas and flaring tempers all around. Montiego remained seated and Luís grinned as Rego escaped, no longer gliding in his desire for haste.

"What was that all about?" asked Luís.

"Get me a brandy, Luís, then I'll tell you. I haven't been this angry since Giuseppe shot Renaldo over his trespassing goats. It is not healthy for my heart."

FOURTEEN

How Luís and Paulo
Come to Trick Margaret Brown

HAVING RECEIVED THE FULL details from
Montiego, Luís concluded his old friend Carlos
was very clever indeed. He envied his cleverness, in fact, and once again felt guilty for his education,
undeserving of it when clearly there were far more
intelligent and worthy persons who would apply
knowledge in useful ways. At twenty-five years of age
Luís believed he really should have accomplished
more, something significant. He measured himself
against boy kings, courageous explorers, his own father
even, who had at least obtained a wife and produced a
son by the age of twenty.

His current position, the result of four years of study,
entailed driving through Albufeira and the neighbouring
villages in his new used van, brightly albeit rather
poorly painted with two sorry-looking beasts adorning

each side and a loudspeaker on the roof, promoting the bullfight with marching music and reminders to the tourists in deliberately over-accented English that, unlike in barbaric Spain, "de bull eez not kilt." The owner of the bull ring eagerly agreed to the cheap advertising campaign, and though it put easy money in Luís's pocket, he couldn't get over the resentment that he was capable of more, was ashamed of participating in the lowest pursuit of tourist dollars.

And then there was guilt, the most stubborn of all the nasty mind creatures, shadowing his spirit. He hadn't enjoyed scholarship, and as a result, hadn't done as well as he knew he could, so now wondered if this was his punishment for that period of slothfulness and false pride. As his grades had deteriorated, his motivation waned, and rather than strive for excellence he skipped classes to lose himself in the university library, scoured the psychiatric texts to find an explanation or excuse for his behaviour. The depth of his ambivalence manifested itself in the subject he chose for his final thesis: "The Conspiracy of Silence." Aware of the impossibility of verification, he proposed that King João II, nicknamed Senhor de Todos Segredos, sent Columbus to the Americas well before the Spanish did. He suggested João's best-kept secret was that Columbus was a Portuguese and a spy, for how could he have successfully found the Americas without the maps and navigational expertise of the Portuguese? His professor passed him on the merit of ambition, national pride and mockery of Spain, but wrote in red marker across the title page: "This is academe, not creative writing! With our great maritime history, there is no need to invent stories."

Luís thought of Carlos's scheme not as a common monetary crime but an act of nationalism. He assumed his friend's motive was purely mercenary, but longed to discuss it with him, or anyone for that matter, in the context of political action. He wished to be back in Lisboa, where intellectual discussions could be found at any time of day or night in one of the Fado houses in the Bairro Alto. He hadn't been a frequent participant in the arguments in those days, didn't really have an opinion to express on the African colonies, Salazarismo, communism. He'd bide his time until the subject of da Gama or Columbus arose, at which point he felt enough confidence to participate. Here in Albufeira, he had only Montiego's conversation, and he wasn't entirely convinced that deep down the man wasn't a fool.

Upon his return from the city, he was confronted with an epidemic of inertia skulking into previously vital spirits. This was not simply a contrast between metropolis and village; his community had given up on their lives. The focus had shifted from sustaining a living in honourable pursuits to acting as indentured servants to the tourists. Proud men cowered before demanding customers in cafés and beautiful young women cleaned rooms while enduring wandering hands briefly flicking and pinching when untethered by the absence of watchful wives. In the heat of the summer, his solitude was stolen and he had begun to resent the tourists as a threat to his personal space, the foreigners for taking up permanent residence as exploiters. He resented them their freedom, their money and their contempt for his people. One night at the disco, drunk and ornery, he'd pretended to shoot them with a cigarette lighter fashioned after a tiny revolver. He smiled and laughed and acted the fool, so no one was offended, but in his heart, he was developing hate.

Essentially, he believed tourism was a demeaning way for a country to exist: prostitution. The best parts of a country should be reserved for its citizens to enjoy, not parcelled off into apartment blocks for English and Germans, worst of all Americans, to visit once a year, or rented back to them, the retornees with saudades, for exorbitant prices.

No country can possibly grow great on the backs of tourists, it is too colonial, with the control of direction clearly in outside hands. How pathetic that a country may be broken by the whim of vacation plans. In peak season, he felt a stranger in his own home, heard more foreign language than his own and developed a yearning for a Portugal for Portuguese — a Portugal for those who love the land, not those who simply wish to use her for a week here and there. She would become diseased by it, a syphilitic whore.

If he were supreme dictator, he would do everything in his power to discourage them. Rather than try to dupe the world into believing Portugal was heaven on earth, he'd create a department of misinformation of a different nature, sending out word of a particular hell. He'd reconvert the castles from hotels into orphanages and schools and museums filled with objects of a proud nation. Surely other countries guard and hoard their best parts, show the rest of the world fabricated amusements: Eiffel Towers, golf courses, theme parks. He would invent violence and crime and disease to keep them away. It would be his own conspiracy of silence, while solitary young men lay on beaches contemplating greatness instead of failure.

"One day we will be hated for occupying our own beaches," he thought. "The more Carlos Pachecos in this land, the better."

He found Paulo throwing sticks along the beach for his dog to retrieve. Paulo could spend entire days in this activity, and Cãozinho, being a puppy still, had the energy and patience for it.

"Olá, Paulo. Bom dia."

"Bom dia, Luís! Watch this!"

He threw the stick into the rough ocean and Cãozinho dove in without fear or hesitation.

"Isn't he amazing?"

"Mmmm. I see you with Cãozinho and am jealous and I do not like to be jealous of you. Will you take me to that woman who has your old place? I hear she has dogs there and I would like to get one of my own."

"Sure, Luís, any time."

"Let's go, then."

"Now?"

"No time like the present."

"I'm sort of busy here, training Cãozinho and all."

"Training him? To do what?"

"Bring back the stick!"

"But that's what they do. That's why they're called retrievers."

"Really?"

Luís shook his head at the total waste of skin before him. "Will you take me or not? If you do, I'll help you train him to do other things."

"Like what?"

"Whatever you want."

"I want him to talk."

"Jesus, Paulo!"

"I was only testing you, Luís, to see if you'd try to trick me. I know dogs can't talk like people."

"Come on, then. Take me out there, before it rains again."

"What's wrong with your new van, anyway?"

"I don't know. Giuseppe's looking at it."

Their loud arrival at the quinta brought six workers out of the villa and caused the dogs to bark and run back and forth in their enclosed area. Paulo immediately went to look at them, and his soothing, gentle words quieted them down.

"Ola!" said Luís to the men. "Is the Englishwoman here?"

"She injured herself and cannot walk. At last, we have peace."

"Why are you still working?"

"What else are we going to do? When the matter is settled, we will be paid by someone. We have a guarantee from da Sousa."

"Does anyone know where the woman is staying?"

"Residencia Montemar."

"Obrigado. Boa tarde. Paulo! Let's go."

Luís recognized her immediately as the fool with the walking stick and inappropriate shoes at the beach, and the thought of her idiocy gave him courage.

"Good afternoon, Senhora. I am Luís Dias da Silva Jr. You know Paulo Pacheco."

Margaret Brown threw her disdain at the boy, as

much for not assisting her at the market as for his familial ties.

"What do you want?"

"We went to Paulo's farm to look at the animals, to see they are taken care of. But since you are with injury, and really not allowed on the property until ownership is settled, I propose Paulo take care of them for you, for a fee, of course. Nothing large, just for his petrol."

Margaret Brown leaned heavily on her walking stick to raise her stature. "I don't know where you lot have gotten the idea that I am made of money, but I assure you I am not. Shame on you for trying to take advantage of a poor old widow."

"Shame on me? It is you, Senhora, who has taken advantage. You are the one who has practically stolen the land from this simple boy. If you step a foot on his property, we shall have you arrested for trespassing. The animals will starve, or perhaps we should set them free, não? Have a feast on donkey meat?"

"You wouldn't dare!"

"Não? But it is very good. You should try it."

Margaret felt her stomach turn.

"Who are you?" she asked quietly.

"I am Paulo's friend and translator. He is a bit of a half-wit and speaks no English, so I am acting on his behalf, protecting him from you and your lawyer, whom I met the other day. I do not like his politics, nor his intentions, and so, I do not like you."

"Well, I don't much care for you either!"

"Good. We are equals, then, in our dislike for one another. You have gone to much trouble for the animals, so I think you do not dislike them. Paulo only requires 500 escudos a day. It is little. And if you agree, we will not tell the men to stop their sneaking work."

Margaret Brown glared at Luís and he smiled back slyly to display victory.

"Paulo, meu compadre," he called. "You are employed."

FIFTEEN

The Pied Piper of the Algarve

PAULO DID NOT RECOGNIZE the perfectly pitched high C squeezed from his brakes as musical, but he liked it and therefore never considered applying oil to eliminate the noise. It drew attention to himself, and one day, as he slowly cruised the hilly streets with nothing better to do, he attracted a small pack of dogs, led by a wiry and grey-haired bitch, the smallest though most aggressive in the gang. One of the dogs limped from a festering gash on its haunch and all were near starvation, so he rolled along and leisurely led them to the controversial quinta. He quickly fed them and introduced the new refugees to the pen of other mutts.

As he sat watching to ensure their acceptance, he remembered snippets of the story of the Pied Piper, but could not recall the details. That evening after supper, when Manny had escaped chores in the sanctuary of Amadeu's, he asked his mother to repeat it for him, not divulging the reason for the request. He dared not discuss his new job with his mother, knowing she would not approve of any association with Margaret Brown. Senhora Pacheco fondly accepted the odd request as just another of his simple ways and told the tale as she recalled it.

"Long ago, in the great city of Oporto, there was much wealth for all and plenty of food on the table. The people were preparing for Easter, planning huge feasts and celebrations, when from across the bridge over the river Douro, thousands and thousands of rats, smelling the food from miles away, invaded the city. They ate up all the food and scared the women and children. The mayor declared he would give five hundred pieces of gold to the person who could rid his city of the rats. A stranger arrived a few days later and told the mayor he could perform the job.

"'Who are you?' asked the mayor.

"'I am called the Pied Piper, because of my colourful jacket and the flute I always play.'

"The mayor told the Pied Piper he would give him the gold as soon as the city was cleared of the rats and the man said it would be accomplished by the next day.

"That evening, the Piper took to the streets and the people could hear him playing on his flute all night long. The rats, enjoying the sound, followed him, and he led them down to the huge river, where they all drowned.

"In the morning, the Piper approached the mayor and asked for his five hundred gold coins.

"'Five hundred?' said the mayor. 'Here, you may have fifty.'

"The Piper said nothing, and left the city. But the next day he returned once more and played a different tune on his flute, and this time attracted all the children to follow him. They danced and ran after the Piper and he led them over the bridge and out of the city forever, leaving very sad and lonely people."

Paulo had forgotten the unhappy ending to the fable.

"Where did the children go?"

"It is a fable, there is no answer," said Senhora Pacheco.

Paulo was not satisfied and figured he'd ask Luís when he saw him.

The next day, Paulo bought a tin flute, one that sounded like, and was perfectly in key with, his brakes. Thus equipped, he sounded like a calliope as he travelled through the village, and with a bag of bones from the butcher fastened to the back of the seat, guaranteed a new set of dogs each time he went out on a mission.

After a week, he'd led a dozen hounds to the farm in this fashion, and when it was time to meet with Margaret Brown, he took her a mental list of names and descriptions. They had arranged to meet once a week at the Hotel Sol y Mar for tea, an update, and to pay him. Paulo did not know Luís had forced the woman to hire him, but she recognized this during their first meeting alone and thought his ignorance could be useful.

With the aid of a guide to dogs from the lending library in Faro, he guessed at the varied lineage of each mongrel. He pointed out the pictures that most resembled the animal and listened while Margaret Brown

told him the name of the breed in English. He
described each personality to her in detail, using single
words she could look up in her pocket Portuguese-
English dictionary: the colour and texture of coats,
size, temperament. His employer was not keen on the
Portuguese names he proposed, but accepted Maria
and Pinto to maintain Paulo's enthusiasm and to garner
good feelings towards herself. Instead, she chose
Minnie for the pack leader, Mona for the howler, Fido
for the Great Dane because he was such a dog, and Dido
for his sister. Sandy was the three-legged retriever of
that colour, Horace (the Horrible) a nasty short-legged
thing of indeterminate breeding and the namesake of a
brother-in-law whom Margaret Brown despised. Once
freed from his initial nervousness, Paulo came to enjoy
these sessions with her and the tea and cakes and slices
she ordered. He believed anyone with such concern for
animals could not be a bad person and personally felt
important and needed by them.

One day as he rode without intending to attract a
pack, going a little too fast for the winding road, a yellow
Lab appeared at his side, running as fast as the motorbike and biting at Paulo's foot, barking. Paulo braked
suddenly and spun out his back wheel, skidded some
distance on the cobblestones before he disengaged
himself from the machine. The dog, tail between his
legs as though he knew what he had done, came and
whimpered and licked at Paulo's face.

"Ai puta. Merda," said Paulo and he swatted at the
dog, which barked and wagged his tail. He looked at
Paulo with beautiful sad eyes that brightened when he
spoke more gently. "I'm okay, boy."

Paulo collected himself and his bike, which was now damaged and wouldn't start. He wheeled it towards the fishermen's beach, where he hoped to find someone who could assist him with repairs. The dog trotted ahead, looking back frequently to confirm direction at a crossroad or to ascertain that Paulo still followed.

Luís intercepted them in the valley road as they approached the square.

"What happened to you? You're bleeding, my friend."

"Ai. This dog," he said. "He chased me. You should have seen him, though, it was very impressive. Twenty miles an hour, I checked. But he was barking and biting at me, so I wiped out."

The dog turned its attention to Luís, and again lowered its tail in a show of submission. When Luís bent down to pet him, he cowered and backed away.

"He looks exactly like the dog I saw in a painting at the Prado. What was it called? *Pero de Chien*, I think, by Goya."

"What does that mean?"

"A dog's fear. Look at him. What's he so afraid of?"

"He's worried I'm angry at him for making me have an accident."

"Não, it's more than that. I think he's been beaten for some time. Look at how scared he is. He can't know he hurt you. Dogs don't have that sort of reasoning ability, only conditioning and response."

Paulo suddenly had an idea that he believed was an excellent one.

"Why don't you take *him*? You said you wanted a dog."

"I lied. I only wanted to get you out to that woman's place to get you a job and trick her."

Paulo frowned. "Ahh. She's really nice, Luís."

"Bah!"

"She is, and so is this dog."

He would never concede on his opinion of Margaret Brown, but Luís had to admit this seemed a particularly nice dog. He had a pretty, pleasant face and occasionally seemed to smile a sly grin. The resemblance to the Goya painting, however, truly intrigued him.

"A dog is man's best friend, Luís. Take him home, and if you don't like him you can give him to me and I will take him to the Quinta dos Angelicus."

Luís grimaced. "What the hell is the Quinta dos Angelicus?"

"My old place, where I work. That is what Senhora Brown has named the farm now that it is a sanctuary for animals."

"Jesus, that's sick. She actually considers herself some sort of angel?"

Paulo stared at the ground and screwed up his face. "She really is, though. And I'm her helper."

"She's a bitch, an imperialist bitch, and she'll take you for a ride if you don't watch out."

"What is imperialist?"

"Taking land that isn't her own. Exerting power over people for her own gain."

Paulo hung his head a little lower and gave his friend a sideways glance. "No one really wanted the farm, Luís."

"That's not the point." He looked suspiciously at Paulo. "You haven't told her that, have you?"

"Não."

"You're certain?"

"Sim."

"Don't ever tell her that."

"I wouldn't. Manny would kill me."

"That's right. At the very least, he'd knock your front teeth out. Now, let's take a look at that bike. Do you have any tools?"

"Não. That's where I was going. Do you know what's wrong with it? Did you learn about motorbikes at university?"

Luís laughed. "Perhaps I should have. At least it would be useful to me now."

The dog tentatively followed as Luís circled the bike to check bits and pieces for loose connections or bolts undone. He occasionally got in the way, and when Luís swatted, he nipped at his hand, not aggressively, just playfully irritating, so that Luís could not get angry.

"Here's the problem," said Luís, pointing to the wire connecting the ignition. "It's come off and all I need is a pair of needle-nose pliers. Go get some from Giuseppe. He's repairing his boat, so should have his toolbox with him."

Once Paulo departed, Luís slapped his thigh as an invitation to the animal and scratched behind his ears the way he'd seen dog owners do. The dog sat still for the attention and after a minute or two his scarlet penis emerged from within its protective sheath. Luís watched as the animal licked the futile erection with vigour.

"Ai! Put that thing away," Luís said, and laughed at how much he sounded like his mother. The dog looked up, grinned, and continued. "We seem to be cut from the same piece of cloth. I guess I have no choice in the matter."

The Bride Price

 CARMINDA BARBOSA HELD a sceptical view of Luisa's repentance and decided the only solution for controlling her uppity daughter was to have her married as soon as possible, to turn her into a problem for a husband and in-laws. Carminda would have preferred to leave her own husband out of it, but to do so would be contrary to all the rules of the Kris, the governing body of the kumpania, and a punishment would be levied on her personally. As far as she was concerned, her husband was soft on the girl, had contributed to her development of disobedience and haughtiness, and he would no doubt wish to make an impossible marriage match based on his ignorance of such faults.

No one with a car wished to risk the journey to Lisboa. The news from the capital was only bad: imprisonment for no reason; torture if a reason could be fabricated; mistrust everywhere so great it was palpable. Of course, pockets were empty and the tourist season was not yet swinging fully enough to justify the trip.

Carminda was forced to take the bus, and it travelled wildly up the windy Lisboa Road, passed slow trucks recklessly and took the sharp bends too quickly. More than once, Carminda believed it would roll over and she threw a curse at the driver to make him slow down. It must have been short of its target, however, as he seemed to increase his speed, while the fidgety youth behind him suddenly calmed down and decided to doze a little. She said a prayer instead and concentrated on the cork and eucalyptus trees as they flew by.

They stopped once during the seven-hour ride to allow the passengers to eat a cod dumpling and use the toilets. Carminda went around to the back of the café to urinate on the ground. She would never use a gadje toilet, and did not wish to be in a small, enclosed space with any of them. The bus was bad enough, and although she was dressed in her city clothes, everyone recognized her as a Cigana and this kept them away. No one sat beside her and she was grateful.

The bus pulled into a park near the river at 8 p.m., too late for her to visit her husband, so she walked to Avenida Augusta where she hoped to find some of her people begging on the wide pedestrian street. She was doubtful, because of the rumours, but the night stretched before her and she longed for some company and a drink. Her small bottle from the bus was dry and the beginnings of a hangover had already crept into the corners of her eyes. Augusta was deserted, so she crossed to the pigeon square and sat at an outside table to survey the few people passing. She ordered a brandy and the waiter requested her money first, with a familiar voice and look that clearly said, "I don't want to serve you, but the night is slow."

A small boy of about five years of age approached with a picture of Our Lady of Fátima, held it out to Carminda with a practiced look of sadness and suffering.

"Where's your mother, child?" she asked in Romany, but this was not a Ciganinho and he did not understand. Angry that she was tricked, she used her fiercest voice on him. "Get out of here," she hissed in Portuguese, "before I put a spell on you to turn you into a dung beetle."

The boy ran away, aware he was in grave danger indeed.

"It is truly a disaster when our livelihood is threatened by the gadje," she thought and wondered where the kumpania should go. Her brandy was set before her and she spoke sweetly to the waiter. "Where is everyone? What is wrong with this city that once couldn't provide enough hours in the day to amuse its citizens?"

"People are nervous. The military is locked up and only the P.I.D.E. are on the streets. Some are talking of a coup, so smart people stay indoors."

"A coup? Who has such big tomatoes to start a coup?"

"General Spínola. Since his book was published, everywhere people are saying it is inevitable and that is why Caetano has put more of his pigs onto the streets."

"Where will it be safe for me to spend the night?"

He laughed.

"Take me home with you and I will put a spell on you to make you the most indefatigable lover in all of Portugal." He laughed again.

"You would be wasting your time, Senhora, for I am that already."

"I will put a love spell on the woman you desire most so that she will be insane only for you."

"She already is, and she is my wife, waiting at our home now for my return. I am afraid I cannot help you."

"Where are the other Ciganos? Surely they have not all left Lisboa."

"Mostly. There's a small shanty town out by the Salazar bridge, and they sometimes come by here, out of habit, I suppose, more than for any purpose." He paused. "If you wait, someone may arrive. I will not hurry you away. I am able to do that."

"Then bring me another brandy if I am to have to sit here alone." What she really thought was, "If I am to sleep outside, I'd rather be drunk and pass out somewhere."

Luís and Spínola
Find Themselves in Trouble

 L U í S DISAPPROVED of leashing a dog to its master, so Paco Vasco da Gama Goya — Paquito when he was good — roamed the streets of Albufeira untethered. His name was a combination of the Spanish painter responsible for his immortalized image and the great explorer, for Paco liked to wander and would often be absent for several days, returning on an early morning to wake Luís for their daily trip to the beach. Their walks included frequent expletives shouted at them when Paco chased after car tires, biting at the smells and speed, and on more than one occasion, Luís adopted an air of dissociation to deflect the drivers' anger.

The dog loved the beach as much as his new master did, and would run its length for the advantage of the wide-open space. His coat bore the exact colours of the sand, so perhaps he also felt safe in his camouflage. Then again, it might simply have been a game, for Luís could easily lose sight of Paco if he lay down or stood in the distance next to the cliff, and he would call out frantically until the animal decided to show himself.

When Luís swam, Paquito ran back and forth at the edge of the sea barking, or lay forlornly waiting for his return. He hated water to such an extent that even rain made him seek cover inside a shop or café, or if none were open he obstinately sat himself in a doorway. Because he belonged to Luís, and was a good-natured, friendly beast who could make himself look like an angel dog, the owners spoiled him with loving attention and whatever scraps they could afford to spare.

It surprised Luís how quickly he developed affection for the dog, and the amount of pleasure he derived from its company. His mother didn't share her son's enthusiasm, for Paco was a thief by habit, and she would frequently discover a piece of meat missing from the counter. Luís hid his amusement, scolded Paco harshly, and to placate his mother, built a dog house in the tiny back courtyard. Once the house was dark, however, Paco would whine at Luís's window until he awoke and brought the animal inside to sleep on the floor beside him.

They were hunting the cats that lived under the snack bar on the beach when Paulo and Cãozinho arrived to play.

"Eh pa!" called out Luís. "How is the working man?"

Paulo was proud to be known in this way, and he grinned. "I am the Pied Piper of the Algarve. The dogs follow me out to the quinta when I play my flute."

"So I've heard."

"Hey, Luís, I forgot to ask you the other day. Do you know where the Pied Piper took all the children?"

"He led the rats out of the city, not the children."

"Não. Remember the end? The mayor didn't pay what was promised, so to get revenge he played a different song to attract the children."

Luís only vaguely remembered this part of the story. "I think I was told he took them to fight against the Moors."

"But they were just children!"

"It's not a true story, Paulo. In all reality, probably many children died of starvation or the plague and the story was made up to tell to the surviving ones so they wouldn't be afraid. That's why those sorts of folktales were told."

"But my dogs aren't going to die or drown, are they?"

"You're taking care of them, não?"

Paulo nodded vigorously.

"Then your story has a happy ending. You are rewriting history, my friend. It doesn't always have to repeat itself. Hey. Blow on your flute and see if you can make the cats come out for the dogs to chase."

"That's cruel, Luís."

"They won't catch them, believe me. Just try it."

Paulo produced a tentative toot, and looked at the snack bar.

"Give me that thing," said Luís, reaching for the instrument, but it was snatched away.

"It's my flute, Luís. I don't want anyone else to use it."

"Fine. Have it your way. Paquito, vem!"

Luís strode down the beach and twice looked back

in anger at his disobedient dog. Paco caught up with him at the top of the wide steps leading to the terrace behind the Hotel Sol y Mar. It was empty of tourists, so Luís sat at one of the tables overlooking the sea. A friend of his worked at the little café, and Luís could count on free cerveja when the manager was not present. He waited a few minutes for service while he cursed Paulo's pettiness, and then impatiently went to find Mário.

He was seated behind the counter, completely absorbed in a newspaper.

"A man could die of thirst out there," said Luís, trying to sound like an irritated tourist.

"Luís!" his friend replied. "Have you heard the news? Spínola has been dismissed!"

"What?"

"Yes, it's right here, an entire two lines devoted to the news. Read for yourself while I get you a copa."

Luís had to search for the brief item amongst the lengthier reports of a loyalty ceremony held to mark the annual celebration of Servicemen's Day. No explanation was provided for the dismissal of both Spínola and General Costa Gomes, chief of staff of the armed forces.

"It's hardly a surprise," said Luís when Mário returned with his glass of beer. "The real question is why Caetano waited so long to do it. What do you think will happen to them?"

"They'll vanish."

Luís considered this. "Não. They can't do that. They're too well known."

"They'll be arrested, then, and sent into exile in a big public display."

"But how, after allowing the book to be published?"

"It makes no sense, I know, unless it was a trap, an excuse to get rid of them."

"Montiego may know what's happening. I'll try to find him." Luís finished his small glass of beer in a quick succession of gulps. "Obrigado for the copa, Mário."

"De nada. Let me know if you hear anything."

"Of course."

As soon as he made a movement to leave, Paco extracted himself from his position under a table, knocking over a chair in his scramble to follow. Luís walked through the tunnel leading towards the square and paused to consider the grafitti along one wall.

"We want a foozball table" it said, and Luís felt ashamed of his juvenile sentiment sprayed in red paint two days ago.

He cut across the square and idle waiters waved and called out friendly greetings. Luís had blocked out the world and heard only his own thoughts, shouting at him to rise up and do something useful. The pulse at his temples chanted "what, what, what?"

The door of the station was locked and he pounded on it in exasperation.

"Ai! Montiego. Wake up and open the door."

It was da Sousa who greeted him, with a sick smile of smugness wrapped around a cigarette butt. Paco bared his teeth and growled softly.

"Montiego sleeps on the job, does he?"

"You'd know better than I. It was only a joke."

"Not a funny one."

Luís shrugged nonchalantly. "Who cares. Is he here? I need to speak to him."

"Não. He's not here. He's working the evening shift."

"Obrigado. Bom dia." Luís waved goodbye and was already a couple of paces down the street when da Sousa called out.

"Not so fast, Senhor."

With his back still turned Luís cursed silently before confronting the officer.

"Sim?"

Da Sousa dropped the cigarette and ground it on the pavement.

"I am told you are harassing Senhora Margaret Brown."

"Then you have been told lies."

"Are you calling me a liar?"

"Of course not. Even if she didn't injure herself, she does not have legal rights to that property. I only reminded her of that and only once. It's hardly harassment. Harassment would be bothering her every afternoon while she eats her cakes at the Hotel Sol y Mar."

"You are outside your bounds, da Silva, you and your pal Paulo."

"We are not outside our legal bounds."

"Let me explain something to you. We have a deep, long-standing allegiance with the British. Margaret Brown has money she wishes to spend in this village. She has friends back in England who will come and visit and spend money in this village. There are people from all over the world who wish to do the same. It is unacceptable for the likes of you and Paulo, people with no means to assist in the progress of the national endeavour, to create an uncomfortable atmosphere for our visitors. It is your job to make them happy, and if you believe you are above such things we can either convince you of the benefits or you can leave, go back to Lisboa and your communist university friends."

Luís knew it was dangerous, but he couldn't control himself. It was the most ridiculous statement ever uttered about himself, and he laughed contemptuously.

"Ai, yi yi, da Sousa. I am no communist. A nationalist, a monarchist, perhaps, sometimes I even think about the benefits of republicanism, but I am not a communist. I wish to get as rich as any of them so I can afford a brand-new villa of my own."

Da Sousa glared. "It will never happen."

"Não?" Luís levelled his gaze, stared directly into da Sousa's eyes. "Watch me."

"Oh, I'll be doing that. Tell me something else, Senhor. What do you know about the murder of the Cigano?"

"Nothing."

"It's funny, that. No one seems to know anything at all. Perhaps someone needs a little boost to his memory."

"I am not a murderer either, da Sousa."

"Não, I do not think you would have it in you, but everyone who knows something and keeps it a secret is accountable."

"I'll be sure to keep you informed if information comes my way. Paquito! Vem. Once again, bom dia, da Sousa."

A different throbbing occupied his temples as Luís returned to the square.

"Fudis, fudis, fudis, fudis, fudis."

He bought a newspaper and went to the nearest table outside to spread it open and read for some distraction. He turned its pages furiously, searching for something of enough interest to stop him from returning to the station and upholding his honour.

"Police Break Up Lisboa Price Protest March."

He looked around for a waiter and waved at a clump of four discussing the football match of the previous day. Luís knew them all, of course, and was greeted with a slap on the back.

"Olá. Boa tarde, Miguel. Um Sagres, por favor."

"And for Paco? Some water?"

"Sim. That'd be great."

Miguel bent down to pat the dog. "I believe there is a ham sandwich in the kitchen that was sent back by a German prick. Would you eat a sandwich touched by a German prick, Paco?"

Luís laughed uneasily. "He is not political, nor racist like you, Miguel."

"But I am not racist. A prick is a prick is a prick. They come in all races."

"So true, even Portuguese," he replied, thinking of da Sousa. "Bring me my beer before I explode."

As soon as it was on the table, Luís drank half, then set it down while he allowed its effects to calm his head. He returned to the article and read.

Three policemen were injured and two youths arrested tonight when strong detachments of security police broke up a demonstration in the centre of Lisboa.

An Interior Ministry spokesman said about 50

young people armed with iron bars gathered in a square and when security forces arrived to break up the crowd, several were injured by flying stones. The crowd was then broken up by baton charges.

A number of the youths, who were apparently demonstrating against the high cost of living, were beaten and clubbed by security forces and plain-clothes agents. The demonstration was organized by the extreme left-wing Proletariat Reorganization Party Movement.

"Right on, brothers," Luís said aloud in English and lifted his bottle in a salute.

He saw Montiego hurrying along the street and shouted, but Montiego couldn't hear above the cacophony of competing music from each café.

"Go get him, Paco," he said and pointed to Montiego. Paco recognized the provider of pigs' ears and bones from the butcher next door to the station, and he ran across the square. The policeman stopped to greet Paco and looked around for his master.

When he reached the table he chided Luís. "Are you so lazy you can't even get up to talk to me yourself?"

"I'm taking an English lesson." Luís held up a finger to silence Montiego while he listened to the chorus about Fernando. "This song, I'm trying to figure it out. I think it's bad luck."

"There's no such thing as a bad luck song. Only bad luck memories from a song."

"I don't know, this one seems to always be around me during bad times. Have you read the news about Spínola?"

"It is disheartening."

"And this?" Luís pointed to the item he just finished.

"Sim."

"What will happen?"

Montiego sat down heavily and motioned to the waiters. Everyone knew Montiego drank vinho tinto almost exclusively, varying only in quantity. A glass was brought and set on the table without an exchange of words.

"The security police can easily suppress such civilian activity. It will come down to who else in the army is prepared to stand behind him."

"Will anyone?"

"People have been given courage by his book." He nodded at the article about the protest. "That is the real crime against the government. We may not like them, but at least they are not stupid men and not quite so fanatical as Franco."

Luís thought of the comparison.

"Caetano isn't really a very good fascist, is he, Montiego?"

"He likely feels in over his head. History will easily forget him and I think he knows that, is trying to find some way to prevent it. Intellectuals don't make very good dictators — they don't know how to abuse power as effectively as the military. President Tomás, however, has training."

"Will there be big trouble?"

"Only if Tomás dismisses him and appoints someone from the very right corner of the military, General Kaulza, for instance, who believes an international communist conspiracy threatens Portugal."

"Does it?"

"That's the million-dollar question, isn't it? I tend to think it is only an excuse for these men to seize power and continue their expensive war games."

"I ran into da Sousa at the station."

"Sim?"

"He accused me of harassment of that Englishwoman, gave me a lesson in Portuguese economics and suggested I go away. He actually thinks *I'm* a communist."

"Keep clear of him, Luís. He is not the brightest star in heaven. However, he does have the power to hurt you."

"He sort of threatened me, suggested I might have information about the Cigano murder which he would be pleased to extract from me, like fingernails."

"Fudis, Luís! I can't protect you if he chooses to."

"What can I do? I've done nothing wrong, really."

"Keep out of trouble and don't find yourself out alone. The whole world seems to be agitated these days, but there are productive actions versus irrational ones. Too many are resorting to the latter. Don't adopt their tactics. And, Luís, if you need to express words, please don't put them on the walls of this village."

EIGHTEEN

Why We Want to Fall in Love
if It's All Just a Bit of Bother

 A YOUNG COUPLE STROLLED across the square, alternately entwined or enfolded into each other as only new lovers feel the need to be, hanging on as if to life itself and displaying their success to the world. They paused at the now-crowded news kiosk to look at postcards, laughed at something that would form part of a fond shared memory, and languished in the simple pleasure of each other's company. The young woman moved with the gentle grace and poise of a cypress tree in the wind, and it was this that held his attention and caused him to stare longingly.

During the too-short time in Luisa's presence, the world around him had suddenly filled up with hope and possibilities and marvels; the ordinary became extraordinary and he felt as though she had smitten him on the head and knocked out a filter around his senses.

When he sat with her at Café Latino, he was the proudest man on earth. He felt that, without looking, he could manoeuvre life's obstacles, that they would be less important, smaller. In her absence, banality became a heavy cloak, complete with a hood to cover his eyes.

"Look at them," he thought to himself. "Even walking becomes a pleasure."

He stroked Paco's head to feel some comfort there. "You have helped, my friend. Walking with you is mostly a pleasure, when you're not a bad dog."

Luís's touch rousted Paco from a lazy slumber, and as he shifted position for additional stroking in more pleasurable locations, he looked across the square and caught sight of a former girlfriend. Without another thought he abandoned the enjoyment of his master's hand, and shot out from under the table and into the crowd.

"Fudis, Paco," shouted Luís, and determined that he would get a leash after all. He watched the two dogs sniff each other, and shook his head at their easy rituals. The bitch suddenly gave Paco a little nip, like a slap across the face for being too forward, and ran through the crowd, Paco in pursuit.

The commotion caused a dispersal of the crowd to territory not inhabited by wild-eyed strays, and the young lovers were once again in his view.

"But it *is* her!" he realized. "With a tourist, and a Spanish bastardo, by his greasy look." His stomach heaved from the poisons of envy, anger and self-pity, experienced with the force of a raging bull against his heart. His first impulse was to attack, and Luís considered the man's size and weight, tried to assess his strength versus the fury inside himself.

Without paying for his cerveja, he got up, slightly drunk by now, and began his approach. The man's hand reached down, carefully lifted a wallet from an open handbag and slipped it into Luisa's large sack. They didn't rush away, but sauntered naturally through the crowd and down a side street.

Luís was more impressed than appalled by the act, its smoothness and professional execution, and his suffering was greatly relieved by the thought of telling Luisa about her lover's nimble fingers. He tracked them down to the pavilion, where they sat on one of the shaded benches overlooking the activity on the fishermen's beach.

"Olá, Luisa."

She looked up and her face contorted.

"Olá, Luís," she sighed.

The man at her side glared, first at Luisa and then at Luís.

"This is my brother, Fernando. Fernando, this is Luís, a person I met swimming."

"Your brother!" Luís thrust out his hand, but Fernando ignored it. "Will the two of you join me for a café?"

Luisa spoke in Romany. "Nando," she said. "I can get some money from this gadjo if you give me fifteen minutes alone with him. You can go and get yourself a drink."

Fernando shook his head, thinking she had learned nothing from her punishment, but he left her alone nonetheless, assuming she would earn the cash in the toilet.

Luís led her to a table outside and ordered two bicas.

"Why didn't you meet me? I have been going insane."

"My mother stopped me. She did this to me." Luisa pointed to her hair with an angry gesture. "So you would no longer want me."

"Why would I care about that?"

Luisa laughed, an edge of hysteria around the sound. "You don't know what you are talking about, Luís. I am a Cigana. I was with a non-Gypsy, and it is forbidden. You are considered dirty."

"Cigana? So that's why your brother stole the wallet."

"You saw that? I'm so ashamed. We don't always steal, but these tourists, they have so much . . ."

"Shh. You don't have to explain. I know. I've considered it myself, in fact. He did it very impressively, actually, and because he is only your brother and not your lover, I don't care. I've thought of nothing but you since we met. I have to see you again, to talk and learn everything about you."

"You are very sweet, but not realistic. My mother is suspicious and I am being watched very closely now. One of our men has been murdered and we will be leaving here very soon."

"That was one of your people?"

"We are all one people. You know something about it?"

Luís lied for the second time that day about his knowledge, and felt sickened.

"I think it was da Sousa. He's D.G.S. and has gone slightly mad from the power."

"Não. It was terrible. A group of villagers came out with shotguns." She paused, recalling the night. "We have an expression in Romany — One madman makes many madmen and many madmen makes madness. There is madness here."

"So run away."

Luisa laughed again, calmer, resigned. "You think I haven't thought of that?"

"We'll run away together. We'll both leave this country before it sinks into the sea from all the rottenness."

"You wouldn't want me, Luís. Trust me. Go find yourself a nice Portuguese girl."

"I don't want a nice Portuguese girl. I want an exotic and beautiful Cigana, if that is what you are."

"It's not so simple. If I leave my family, choose to live apart from the Ciganos, I am no longer a Cigana. Do you understand? I abandon that, and I abandon who I am. There is no going back, for I will be mahrime — dirty — and a traitor."

"All I ask is that you consider it. Take as long as you need, see me when you can, but don't dismiss the possibility."

Fernando returned and lurked about, leant on a pillar in the shade and kept an eye on his sister. Whatever she was up to, he held responsibility, and had no intention of incurring his mother's fury one more time.

Luís glanced over, to make sure he wouldn't be overheard.

"Please, meet me so we can talk. I can help you however you wish. I would kill for you, steal for you. Anything."

She studied his face as though it might provide an answer.

"Tomorrow. If you have a few escudos, I might be able to bribe my brother."

"How much?" he asked, reaching into his pocket. He pulled out a bill and some coins. "I have 500 escudos."

"That should be enough. Where?"

"It's a secret beach, where we can be private. Do you know the fishing shack, through the field across from where the market is?"

Luisa nodded.

"There's a small path to the left. Follow it and you'll come to the beach. I will wait for you all day, from the moment the sun begins to warm the shore until it colours the heavens magenta."

"I will try again, but please do not be angry if I'm not able."

A Suitable Match

 PRISON WAS TOLERABLE for Zlato Barbosa, owing to an affable nature and a multiplicity of talents demonstrated to entertain his guarders and fellow inmates. His vaudevillian act comprised lively songs, dances and, in particular, skilful feats of knife throwing. A truculent miscreant would be summoned into the small courtyard and made to spread his limbs against the wall. He was not afforded the luxury of being bound, and a flinch, however slight, invited the six-inch blade to pierce his flesh. On occasion, the target would, in fact, be wounded as a result of Zlato's fallibility or a 500-escudo note found in his room before a scheduled performance. A 1,000 note ensured the knife landed in the stomach and Zlato would wring his hands afterwards, muttering to observers of too much vinho the night before. Such

notes had been appearing regularly over the past two
months and he was beginning to be irritated by the
threat to his reputation as a superb marksman, but
knew if he regained his accuracy, his usefulness would
diminish. There were plenty of other Ciganos in the
jail, any of whom would eagerly replace him.

Zlato's crime was being a Cigano, and as a Cigano,
unable to produce the required identity documents
demanded of everyone these days. The D.G.S. was man-
dated to corral all potential subversives and foreigners
without proper cause for being in the country. The
Ciganos posed a particular dilemma, for without documents the officials didn't know where to send them. A
systematic expulsion to the Angolan area had proven
ineffective, for a well-established and welcoming Cigano
community existed there, established more than 250
years earlier during King João V's aggressive extermi-
nation program.

History is vague on the root of the particular ani-
mosity that caused that king, in 1718, to order increased
efforts to rid his kingdom of its Gypsies, but the collapse of a long and passionate affair with a beautiful
Cigana was rumoured to have caused him such angst
that he wished to banish, and punish, them all. They
were rounded up under unjustifiable anti-Gypsy
statutes, scattered through the separate conquests of
India, Angola and Brazil. The governor in Angola welcomed the emigrants, who adjusted most favourably to
the climate and proved the more law-abiding of all the
colonists.

Amongst the prisoners with Zlato, not a single Cigano
had committed a criminal offence, and while many of

the Portuguese had not either, the Ciganos felt particularly vulnerable.

It was very early in the morning when a guard rousted him with unusual camaraderie, using his nickname rather than a pejorative.

"Ai, Lamino, your bitch is here."

If there is a common bond between men of all races, it is a sympathy over the existence of a domineering wife. No matter how great an enemy, if he is an unlucky son of a bitch in this respect, he deserves the smallest kindness from his brothers. Zlato's heart was not gladdened at the news of his visitor. His wife's absence from his days had done much to improve his overall demeanour.

"Hello, Zlato," she greeted him in Romany. "Is fate treating you well?"

"Speak Portuguese, woman. They don't like foreign language here. They may think we're plotting a grand scheme and would feel obligated to torture me. Why have you come?"

"It is about your daughter. It's time for her to marry. She begins to wander and I suspect she has been meeting with a gadjo in the village. We must discuss her bride price and suitable husbands."

"How have you let her meet this gadjo?" he asked, shaking his head in disbelief. "What a disgraceful mother you are."

"She is spirited, Zlato. Not even you would be able to stop her."

"Pfff. She would not defy me. Why didn't you bring her so I could speak to her?"

"It's too dangerous in Lisboa. We're all being arrested

and she is so pretty, she'd surely draw attention to herself. If she was arrested we'd never see a bride price. She would be mahrime completely."

Zlato had to agree, for he heard regularly of the particular punishment of female prisoners.

"There's a man who was here briefly before he paid the right person, José Rabelo. Find him. He's as rich as any man in Portugal. He comes from Spain but is thinking he'd like to stay now in Portugal because their Franco is worse even than Salazar was. I spent many happy hours describing Luisa's beauty to him, and though he denied interest in marriage, I'm certain he is considering the advantages."

"What price do you set?"

He thought for a moment. "There is no price. He saved my life in here when I accidentally killed an important member of the Portuguese mafia, so he has already paid. I shall give him Luisa as a gift of gratitude."

"But it's a great deal of money. I don't mean disrespect, but perhaps you are unaware of how difficult it has become for us to earn a living. How can I pay for a wedding celebration and feast?"

Zlato removed one of his boots and pulled out a compressed bundle of notes, stinking with six months of contact with sweating feet.

"Use this. Tell her to visit me with José after the wedding. Now I must go or else I won't get my breakfast."

He left her there peeling the notes apart and counting them.

A Hiccup

 TO MONTIEGO, IT SEEMED ironically typical of Portugal's long-suffering and pathetic accep-tance of submission that the man lighting the spark of revolution was a sixty-four-year-old general. He wondered whether the world was paying attention to Spínola and what it thought of his dichotomous persona. Should the esteemed members of the world media take the time to do a little research, they would discover he had fought in the Spanish Civil War on Franco's side and received both his training and his habit of wearing a monocle from the Wehrmacht in Nazi Germany. And if they discovered that, would they bother reporting that as governor general in Guinea-Bissau from 1968 to 1973, he had attempted to counter insurgency there with social reform and a wide range of community projects? The man Montiego knew from his own days in the army was a tough fighter who never held back from combat and was highly respected by his troops. He returned to Portugal a hero among the military and general populace, an indisputable patriot, but Montiego worried that an inept foreign government would interfere on Premier Caetano's behalf, fearing Spínola's past associations and ignorant of his direction, his stature and the true significance of this most spectacular accomplishment.

When Caetano himself read a prepublication copy of his book, confiscated from the publishing house, he understood that the military challenge that he could sense had been coming was inevitable. Junior officers within the military were already in a rebellious mood over low pay and poor conditions, and for the past three weeks, his informants had reported unrest amongst a small group, resulting in the blanket confinement of the lower ranks to their barracks.

The premier tended to agree with Spínola's proposals to end the conflicts in Africa, and the prospect of positioning himself at the helm of a vast, united Lusitanian community of Brazil, Portugal, Angola, Mozambique and Guinea-Bissau appealed to his sense of personal grandeur. He had allowed the book to be published to open up the debate a little, without dirtying his own hands, and to avoid a clash with the army. It was a game of chicken, using Spínola against the president and his ultra-right establishment, resulting in extreme pressure from that quarter to sack Spínola, and Costa Gomes for endorsing the blasphemous volume.

Depression overwhelmed Montiego when he read his morning newspaper; an immediate exhaustion of body, mind and spirit. Two days earlier, it was reported, officers loyal to Spínola met secretly in their barracks to devise a plan of protest. In Caldas da Rainha, forty miles north of Lisboa, a group arrested their own commanding officer, locked him in a cell and proceeded in a convoy of armed trucks towards the capital. They expected reinforcements along the route and to amass final support in Lisboa, but the men were quickly intercepted by faithful troops of the Caetano regime. The old order, immutable, barely quivered. It was as though Caetano, President Tomás, the entire establishment, hiccuped and relaxed.

Montiego wasn't fond of Harry Young, in part for his involvement with Senhora Brown, but more as a result of a lingering suspicion that all Englishmen are loutish drunkards, a prejudice sprung from horrific tales of their behaviour during the crusades against the Moors. He thought he could tolerate the man's arrogance for the duration of a copa at his tacky pub.

"Olá, boa tarde, Montiego. Como va isso?" Harry called out vigorously, not entirely sincerely and with suspicions of his own.

"Life is complicated, Harry."

"What? Even in the Algarvian paradise?"

"It is difficult to think, I know. I come to read your English newspapers, to uncover what happens around us."

Harry looked Montiego straight in the eyes and lied easily. "I don't have English newspapers. That would be contrary to the censorship rules."

Montiego was prepared for the denial, expected no less of an intelligent foreigner. It was a dance, a game played between authority and public without any rules or pattern. Montiego didn't enjoy the game, preferred established and consistent rules, but he was adept nonetheless.

"Your papers are read in Lisboa before they come to you. The government saves a few escudos. They determine it is an acceptable chance to allow you to read them, pero, you are on our little list at the station."

Harry considered whether this was a trap, revenge against him for his role in Margaret Brown's land dispute. He too was astute, and knew enough about Montiego to step towards cooperation.

"I hear you are a man of honour," he said, unable to keep sarcasm away from this final word. "Do I have your word that your interests do not rest with any infraction on my part?"

"You have my words."

Harry went to the safe in his office and retrieved his collection of *The Times* from the past few weeks. They were neatly folded and uncreased, a precious connection to be treated with respect.

"Here's a nice bit of good news. Iberia Airlines will serve free Spanish wine on all its flights."

"It is not time for joking. I am most anxious if there are news of Spínola."

"Some. We tend to believe Caetano has become tolerant of fresh ideas. There is speculation that he must favour Spínola's proposals, or he would not have allowed the publication of the book."

"So why is he dismissed?"

"Do you blithely believe Caetano actually has power? He is no Salazar. Tomás makes the decisions. Premier

Caetano played a dangerous move allowing the book to come out. He too is in peril of dismissal."

"How do you know?"

"There are important English interests in Portugal and in Africa, so we must know how they may be affected, protected. There is cooperation."

"Do they report of the regime's crimes against people?"

"They have no idea, or they don't care. Probably the latter, for there are more serious troubles at home. The press is consumed with other matters. The IRA is terrorizing England. Oil prices and the embargo. Beirut. President Nixon's indiscretions. Portugal and Angola do not hold much interest for anyone. Canada sends aid to the rebels and the U.S. is wary of entering another conflict so will not lift the embargo on the use of its weapons in Africa. I'm not certain they are taken seriously, your colonial wars. They do not affect anyone of *significance*."

"Pridefully alone, with only white supremes in South Africa for support. No one wishes for our equal society or a united Lusitanian power."

Harry chortled. "Portuguese power. It is an anachronism."

"Please?"

"Portuguese and power: it is in the wrong time."

"Obrigado, Harry. I will read your papers myself and return them when I finish. Also, I advise you to be most vigilant in the futuro. When you hear your BBC broadcasts, I propose you close the windows. The lane is polluted by English voices, and someone can complain. We would be obliged to investigate matters."

"Of course. I am sorry to have disturbed the good residents."

TWENTY-ONE

The Master of Amor

A FINE MIST, its moistness like dewy fairy kisses, blew across the tiny beach, as though the sea was airborne, her nymphs jumping up to beckon him to come play in its depths. He turned his face to receive it directly, closed his eyes and brought it inside him, to become him. With his eyes closed, the smell was fresher, the undulatory rhythms of the waves more acute: what he imagined to be the perfect tempo for making love. He must remember to listen for it, to allow it to guide him towards ecstasy rather than become overwhelmed by the much anticipated event. Luís was determined to be an exceptional master of love, given the opportunity. It might make up for all the failures and doubts.

He considered this beach his, and most of the time it was — a beach made by the gods for the pleasures of two, sheltered, private, accessible only if you knew the tides. He frequently picked mussels off the rocks, always small here, the way he liked them, and took them home for his mother to cook in white wine and garlic. In the summer he came to avoid the crowds, as tourists seldom explored, preferring the easy and obvious, water closets and cold cervejas on hand, so the only people Luís ever met were his neighbours, and they had no time for the beach but on weekends and festas. He came to be naked, to dream of the day he would bring a woman and make love all day in the sun and the sea, like one of da Gama's sailors with his gift from Venus.

The water in March was cold enough still to make his tomates retreat into his body. He always recalled the first time it had occurred, when he ran crying to his father, believing it was a permanent disfiguration.

"Warm them with your hand and they will come back like magic," he'd responded with affection. The fear never quite left Luís that he'd be stuck with a pair of shameful tomates no bigger than those grown in pots, and he developed a habit of checking them regularly, whether freshly chilled or sticking to his thigh with sweat.

He took a long swim to ease his anxiety, allowed the sun to dry his body and then moved into the shade of the cliff when the sun reached its burning apogee. He lay his head on his arms for a siesta and in the semiconscious state before sleep came, he wandered for the first time in weeks to the blissful kingdom of the imagination. His mind freed itself of the intrusion of reality and took him to the places he knew he belonged but couldn't quite reach within the tethers of existence.

When Luisa cast her aura onto his body, there were no gravitational effects of decorum to control him. She giggled at the sight of his little penis, a wee, bird-like creature asleep in a thick nest of hair. It wobbled three or four times and gradually grew into something different entirely, and for some moments she studied it, considered its cleverness, before going to the ocean for an antidote.

Luís was startled by the water sprayed on his belly and it required an effort to accept he hadn't fallen into the sea but, worse, had been lying with an erection in the girl's presence.

"How long have you been here?" he asked.

"Long enough," she replied, and something in her face caused him to blush.

"We are even now, then," he said. "I shouldn't be embarrassed."

"Não. Clothes are only needed by vanity, I think."

"Then I'm afraid I am vain," he said, and pulled on his shorts as he stood to greet her properly. "Olá, Luisa."

"Olá, Luís."

He smiled at the repetition of their names and how it made him feel they were two halves waiting to be fit back together.

"I'm pleased you were able to come."

"Sim."

He reached for her hand, brought it to his mouth to kiss, and his gesture of romance was thwarted by the presence of an elaborate ring of sapphires, emeralds and rubies on her index finger. Luís had not seen it before, and its brilliance intimidated him.

"That ring. It is so beautiful. Where did you get it?"

"It's been in my family for hundreds of years."

"Hundreds? You do not exaggerate a little?"

"Not at all. Do you wish to hear the story?"

"Please."

"It's quite long."

"I have all the time in the world for you. Here, share my towel."

"The sand does not bother me." She easily folded herself into a cross-legged position next to his towel, and Luís pushed it aside before affecting a casual pose in the sand himself.

"Okay. So a Moorish king was in the woods hunting with a servant when a big storm moved in, blowing down trees and raining so hard, it hurt the skin. They went in search of shelter and came across a charcoal burner and asked for lodging for the night in return for payment of a very large sum. The kind little man agreed and put the king and his companion in his own bedroom. During the night, the king was awakened by a loud moaning from the courtyard where his hosts slept, followed by a voice from nowhere which said to him: 'A child born at midnight shall be your wife. No matter what you do, what suffering she may cause, you cannot escape your fate.' This bothered the king a great deal and he stirred his sleeping servant for consolation. They put it down to a bad dream, for the servant heard nothing, and went back to sleep. In the morning, the king asked the charcoal burner what all the noise was about in the night.

"'My wife gave birth to a daughter at exactly midnight,' he said. The king remembered the voice and the prediction and quickly said to his host: 'I am a king and have much money. I can raise your daughter in the best circumstances. I will pay you for her in gold which I have here with me.' The charcoal burner consulted with his wife and agreed to the deal. They were very poor and couldn't afford another mouth to feed.

"The king and his servant were five miles from their resting spot when they happened upon a river. 'Take the child and drown her in the river,' commanded the king. The servant didn't have the heart to kill an innocent child, so he fastened her blanket around her with his own sash and hid her among the brambles.

"She was discovered by a gentle fisherman who had come to the bank of the river and, since his wife could not have children of her own, he took the infant home and named her Maria of the Brambles.

"Several years later, the king and his loyal servant were once again touring the countryside and stopped in a little village by the river where Maria was abandoned. It was a festa and all the people of the village were celebrating in the square, dancing and eating and drinking wine. The servant noticed an exceptionally beautiful child with a red sash around her waist. Upon closer inspection, he identified it as his own belt and concluded that this was the same child, quite miraculously alive. He informed the king, admitting that he hadn't killed the infant, and was told he must do it this time. The king approached the new parents and again offered a large sum of money to take their beautiful daughter to the palace to be raised as a princess. The couple loved Maria very much and were sad to lose her, but believed the king would give her a wonderful life, so agreed.

"The servant built a small wooden coffin, placed

Maria in it and threw it in the river. The current was strong and it carried the coffin several miles out to sea, where it was discovered by a fishing boat. The men hauled the box aboard and were delighted to find such a beautiful little girl, alive, inside. They returned to port in Spain and news quickly spread of the find. It was such an exceptional story that their queen wished to take care of the child, and brought her into her court to be a companion for the princess.

"When it was time for this princess to marry, all sorts of kings and queens and nobles were invited to the celebration. Our king and his servant attended, and the night before the great ball, there was a large reception for all the guests. When Maria saw the king, she approached him, confronted him and, using the very same words he'd heard on that night fifteen years earlier, announced that she would be his queen. The king immediately panicked. He gave her a ring he'd brought with him to present to a different lady at the wedding and said, 'Wear this ring and dance with me tomorrow evening. With this ring. We shall wed. Without it you shall die.'

"Maria was disturbed by these words, and fled to her room. In the night, the king had his servant break into her bedroom, steal the ring and throw it into the sea. When Maria awoke in the morning, the ring was gone, and she was afraid she would be killed that night. She went to the kitchen to get breakfast for the princess, and the cook was cleaning several fish for that night's banquet. Maria saw something flash in the light from the window, and there in the fish's stomach was the ring.

"That evening, when the king asked her to dance,

he recited the words from the day before. Maria pulled the ring from the bodice of her dress, slipped it on her finger and said in reply: 'I am your queen, was born to be your queen, and regardless of hardship you cannot escape your fate.'

"There. That is the story of the ring. This is that same ring, passed down for hundreds of years until now."

"And you believe this story?"

"Why shouldn't I?"

"I studied the history of this country at university for four years, and history doesn't bear it out."

"Whose history? What remains of Moorish history before your slaughter of them? And the story of the Roma? Our history has never been recorded. Too few of us read or write."

"I'm sure some has survived."

"Yes, and the stories are told to children such as myself around campfires by our grandparents. Just because it isn't in your fancy university libraries doesn't mean it didn't happen."

"Não, but it sounds like a fairy tale to me, concocted to justify the existence of that ring, no doubt stolen from someone."

"That is a very arrogant statement, made, I think, by someone who has no right to arrogance. I believe it. It means I am a princess and I want to believe I am a princess."

"A princess? And you are treated as such?"

"My mother is only jealous. I don't believe she is really my mother, because she has never worn the ring."

"And what does it mean? Do you have royal obligations?"

"I am supposed to marry one of the best of my people and produce many, many children so our race survives."

"And if you don't?"

"I must pass on the ring and relinquish the title of princess. I would be cast out of the kumpania."

"If it doesn't get you anything but mistreatment and too many children to feed, why would you want it?"

"It makes me feel special."

"But you are without it."

"No, I'm not. I'm just another thieving Cigana, não?"

"I didn't say that."

"You didn't have to. I know what people think of us. I'll have to leave this country if I want to escape that, this continent even. North America is probably the best place. I hear there are so many different races there, all marrying one another, a new one is created every time a child is born. Canada is supposed to be particularly welcoming of every sort of people, as you have said."

"I don't want you to go anywhere. You're the first woman I've ever felt comfortable with. When I'm with you, I feel like a jigsaw puzzle that has been completed. You can be my princess, treated as such for as long as I live."

"If I stay here much longer, I think I might give up, accept my destiny and marry one of my people."

"How do you know what your destiny is? You are a fortune teller?"

"Of course I am."

"Then tell me what my fate is."

"Give me your hand."

Luisa took it in hers, and the simple act of her touch, her gentle caress, sent shivers through his arm.

"It will still be many years before you find the love you seek. You have other, more important matters to attend to in your life before you are able to concentrate on love. It would get in the way and prevent you from achieving your destiny. Once you find it, however, it will be for a very long time and you will be happier than you ever imagined possible. If you deny yourself this destiny, and rush into love before its time, you will experience constant disappointment in life until you finally achieve your true destiny."

"And what is that destiny?"

"Only you can discover that. You must find it, for the journey is part of it."

"How do I find it?"

"See all of these lines here? These are all false starts, many of which you have already experienced. You must keep trying new things until one feels right. If it feels right, you must not let it go, you must not allow yourself to be afraid or discouraged."

"But you feel right."

"You are a man. I am a woman. That is what you are feeling. We can enjoy this day together, and not say goodbye, but have a beautiful memory of friendship to carry around with us for the rest of our lives. And if it is our fate, we shall meet again when the time is right."

"If I had paid you for that, I would demand my money back and have you arrested for being a fake."

Luisa laughed. "Do you always hear what you wish to hear?"

"Never. That's the problem. Please, Luisa. Think about it. I can give you a better life."

Luisa sighed. "Let's take a walk."

"You are not afraid of being seen?"

"Não."

"Where do you wish to go?"

"Show me something special to you."

Luís's mind was still preoccupied with the thoughts of a twenty-five-year-old virgin. He'd attempt to lure her into the cave one more time, to obtain a kiss at the very least.

"We have to go back to the main beach and follow the path along the sea. It's calm enough today to not be dangerous."

Luisa stood and brushed the sand from her bottom. Her action stirred Luís once more, and he cursed under his breath.

"May I hold your hand as we walk, Luisa? Will you give me that small pleasure?"

She extended hers towards him and together they made their way back along the road to the beach. Luís pointed out his favourite things to her: the storybook cacti flowering with what looked like a ten-foot asparagus spear; wildflowers growing out of the cracks in plaster houses; the stunning view of the old village from a particular bend in the road; and the blessed hands of Fátima cast in iron to knock on the doors of the old cottages. Luisa took in his observations and tried to summon the same enthusiasm for place.

"You really love to be here, don't you?"

"Of course! It is my home. My country. Don't you?"

"You forget who I am. I belong to no country."

"But don't you have a favourite? Is this not it?" He made a sweeping gesture with his free hand.

"There is no sense in having a favourite."

"That is the saddest thing imaginable to me."

Luisa shrugged slowly. "You will always be Portuguese, whether you are in Portugal or not. If you leave your beloved country, you will not lose who you are and you will always be able to return. We have no country, only what we call the Lungo Drom, the long road leading nowhere. We are everywhere, but we are only ourselves, citizens of no nation."

"But surely you could choose to be a citizen."

"Who'd take me?"

"Is it as bad as that?"

Luisa released her hand from his and stopped walking to look him straight in the eye.

"You, and everyone like you around the world, see only poor, begging creatures. You do not think we have any right to our customs or our survival. You try to force us into work we do not wish to perform, make it illegal for us to travel, to tell fortunes. We were thrown in the ovens, you know, but only the Jews get any sympathy, like it was acceptable for us. We are evicted from every country. If we settle, our homes are burnt down, and if we don't, we are told we cannot park our caravans. We have been murdered, imprisoned, sterilized only for who we are."

"I'm sorry."

"It's not your fault, is it?"

"Não, but I too have had bad thoughts towards your people." He held his head in his hands for a few moments, hit his temples harshly. "I knew some people were going to your encampment. I did nothing to stop them."

Luisa stared silently out at the sea.

"Say something. Tell me how terrible I am. Anything."

"Why did they do it? What did he do?"

"He might not have done anything, but they believe it was one of your men who raped and killed a little girl."

"Do you believe that?"

"Não, but I'd prefer to think someone of my own race and religion is incapable of it."

"Whatever others think of us, we are very religious people. We don't rape and we don't kill. We don't mind the misconception so much, really, as long as you leave us alone. We actually try to make you fear us. It is a power. Your approval isn't necessary, only your tolerance."

"Can you forgive me?"

"I can learn whether you are a good person or a bad person. Is that the same?"

"I believe it is." Luís's amorous thoughts had retreated behind self-loathing and he was greatly relieved to spy Paco running up the road towards them.

"Paquito, meu cãozinho. Excuse me, Luisa, here is my dog."

Paco barked at Luisa and showed his teeth.

"See, even your dogs hate us."

"Não. He's only jealous of you. Stop it, Paco," said Luís and swiped at his head. The dog growled, less fiercely, and took a few sniffs of the girl, but his attention was diverted by the sound of a car. As soon as it came into view, he was off again, in a frenzy of barking.

"He was a stray and so not very well behaved. I'm sorry."

"Why do you apologize for an animal? You seem to apologize for everything."

"Love is always having to say you are sorry."

Luisa did not catch his clever turning around of a popular sentiment.

"Who wants it, then?" she said.

He took her hand again and continued walking.

"Have you put some sort of curse on me that causes me to be ill when you're not with me?"

Luisa laughed. "It wasn't necessary, I think. You are doing it to yourself. I wouldn't waste a curse on something I could achieve by other means."

When they arrived at the promenade overlooking the beach, Luís looked around to ensure they would not be seen by anyone he knew, not out of embarrassment, but he didn't want to be followed by an envious acquaintance intent on sabotaging his fantasy.

"Come, I will take you now to one of my favourite places."

A path had been formed by thousands of feet moving boatless fishermen to tranquil locations. The rains had eroded the coastline so at times it disappeared entirely and they had to walk on stony, uneven ground.

"I haven't been along here in a while. It was once a very easy walk."

Luisa didn't doubt this, but questioned their sensibility in the present. She was about to suggest returning to the safe, wide stretches of flat shore when Luís announced their arrival.

"Here we are. This was my fort when I was a boy, used as a base from which to fight imaginary invaders." He led her into a large cave, lit from its deepest recesses by a hole in the roof.

"You could live in here," said Luisa, impressed by the practicality of nature.

"I used to imagine I did. Once I spent the night, well, tried to spend the night, but was frightened off by a snake. Sit."

Luisa looked at him with raised eyebrows.

"It's fine. Really. That was the only time I ever saw an animal in here. Here. There is a log we can sit on."

They sat and Luís pulled out his cigarettes, offered the package to Luisa.

"I don't smoke."

"Too bad. It's highly pleasurable, particularly during times of stress. The day I waited for you, the day you didn't come, they provided my only solace."

"Now *I* am sorry. Tell me something about the Portuguese, a story of your history and what makes you so proud and angry at once. Tell me something that will make me consider it would be better to be with you."

"Where do I begin? The first great Portuguese triumph was over the Moors, in 1267 after almost two hundred years of fighting. With them out of the way, the kings could concentrate on other matters, and they turned their attention to finding a sea route to the East, for untold riches awaited the country that could secure direct access to the source of spices, the most sought-after commodity of the Middle Ages."

Using a stick, he scratched a crude drawing of Europe, Africa and India in the dirt, the Iberian Peninsula unwittingly and grandly out of proportion.

"In 1415, Henrique el Navigador established a centre for maritime research and exploration down the road at Lagos, and by the time he died in 1460 the West African mainland was known quite well. Madeira, the

Canary Islands and the Azores had all been colonized. These accomplishments caused successive kings to continue the quest for a trade route, new colonies, and to expand the Christian faith, of course.

"The culmination of a hundred years of courageous maritime endeavours occurred in July 1497, when Vasco da Gama and 170 men departed from Lisboa. Fogs and storms, conflicting currents and contrary winds made the journey very dangerous. They met Arab traders who were interested in seeing them fail in their mission, and in Mozambique and again in Mombasa they narrowly escaped death. Finally, in May of 1498, they anchored off Calicut, in India, after ten and a half months at sea."

He added the coastlines of a diminutive North and South America a short distance from his epicentre, and drew a weak line across.

"Columbus's adventures to the New World have dominated the record of history, but at the time da Gama's discovery was considered far greater. The spices and precious stones he brought back from India resulted in the emergence of Portugal as the richest, most powerful nation in all of Europe.

"We took Brazil, were the masters of the Indian Ocean, Persian Gulf and the Red Sea. But thousands of lives were lost and it was an incredible drain on the country's very limited population. No one really knew at what cost their empire had been built. In 1578, King Sebastião ordered a crusade to North Africa, and within two years Portugal and all her empire had fallen into the lap of Spain. We recovered our independence in 1640, but had lost our place in the world forever."

Luisa sat quietly trying to understand the concepts of conquest and crusade. The desire for trade and wealth was simple, but the ownership of people and land was not familiar.

"And what about now, today?"

"History is repeating itself, our leaders wasting all our money and strong young men fighting to hold on to territory, to control people."

"This is what makes you angry?"

"Partly, yes. I do not want to lose my life or a limb fighting for something I don't care about. It is wrong, but I do not consider fighting in Angola to be defending Portugal. I only wish to build something for myself, a family and a living, here at home, and that is not so simple these days."

"Family is most important among my people, because we have no country of our own. Maybe now you can understand my hesitation. Our goals are similar, but whereas you do not necessarily worry about your bloodline it is all we have."

"Is it important? Is it more important than your own happiness?"

"It should be. Our biggest accomplishment is surviving as a persecuted, hated race wherever we are. Perhaps one day, several hundred years from now, our ability to survive will make us a great people, the only ones able to survive what the world has in store."

As she studied Luís's map, she felt pride and anger for the plight of her people, picked up her own stick and used it to mark their territory, added Eastern Europe and Russia.

"We have a presence in every country in the world,

you know. We go to a country and exist, not by over-powering the people, not killing them or enslaving them, but we have established settlements nonetheless and perhaps that is an even greater accomplishment than yours. Have you ever thought about that?"

"You are so smart and beautiful and fascinating, Luisa. You can teach me so much, and in return, perhaps there is something I can give to you. Please, will you see me again?"

Luisa wondered if what he could give her would ever be enough.

"If I do, I want you to bring me proof that you are seeking your place in the world. There is no point otherwise or you will become bitter and mean and ugly and eventually blame me for it."

"Never!"

"That is my condition."

"Then I agree."

"Okay. Now, I must get back. Thank you for showing me this cave." She rose and Luís scrambled off the log.

"May I kiss you goodbye?"

"I would like that."

His kiss was tentative and gentle, his lust supplanted by an instinct to move cautiously. He held her to him for a moment to allow her the experience of feeling protected rather than merely desired.

TWENTY-TWO

Luís Joins the Ranks of Great Portuguese Writers

 LUÍS CONSIDERED the histories not included in books as he sat on a rock waiting for his rod to quiver and bend with a reward for his patience. A soft lapping sound complemented the calm around him, as though the sea herself could not summon up the energy necessary to create a proper wave. The water was so clear and still, a man could be tricked into believing all he need do was reach down and grab his lunch. He wondered how many men had succumbed to such illusions.

His own father, for starters, tricked into believing the answer for his son lay in education, that Salazar's "New State" would restore the country to its proper rank in the world.

Luís da Silva Sr. considered Salazar a saviour, and his son had adopted the paternal position. Many students at the university had spoken of suppression of speech, rumours of torture and imprisonment, but Luís hadn't been interested. He wanted only to secure for himself a position in the new Portugal as promised by Salazarismo. But after forty-eight years of "God, Country, Family," they were now the poorest country in all of Europe, shamefully behind Spain even, and Caetano spent all their money on the futile wars in Africa.

Three forces were at work to motivate Luís. Shame is a powerful motivator, one that can paralyze the strongest man, and it bore down on him, caused his shoulders to slump forward slightly, his feet to shuffle as though the weight of his failures pressed him towards the earth. He was ashamed of himself as a historian, blinded by his own arrogance and challenged by an uneducated Cigana. The Moors hadn't interested Luís in school because they were the losers and no one is much interested in losers. He was shamed that he had thought nothing of the murder of the Cigano, had not even questioned its validity.

Love was at work, his heart sending constant messages to his brain to prove his worthiness to Luisa by acknowledging her history and recording it as a gift to her. If he could accomplish this task, perhaps she would reconsider the necessity of bearing too many children to keep her race alive. It could live in the pages of his book instead. Her family might see his worth in it also, and bless their union. He would rectify his past failure as a scholar by creating a valuable missing link in the history of his country.

Finally, there was Spínola. His book was the biggest seller in Portuguese history and the strong reactions of both the government and the people proved the effect well-written pages are able to produce. Spínola had the government scared, the establishment angry, officers prepared to fight for his honour, and the people, finally, hopeful of an end to the morass they had endured for two generations.

"After all," he thought, "my thesis was a fine piece of creative writing."

He was embarrassed at the papelaria selecting a notebook to begin his scratchings. The young man behind the counter eyed him and said unpleasantly: "We have a new Spínola right here in Albufeira, do we?"

Luís fumbled to pull a few escudos from his pocket.

"I'm learning advanced English, actually. It is the language of the future."

"Not my future," said the clerk with contempt.

Luís shrugged. He felt the same way, of course, but it was an easier ridicule to accept because it was untrue. Beside the counter, a display of fountain pens and an assortment of inks spoke to him of beautiful words and Luís felt he had to have one.

"How much are they?" he asked, pointing.

"Five hundred escudos."

Luís looked again and thought of the groceries he was meant to bring home, the fish he'd have to buy since he'd abandoned the exercise of catching one. His mother could work her magic on salt cod, bacalhão, the faithful friend, one more time.

"That one," he said, picking out a sleek black pen with a silver nib. "And bright blue ink to fill it."

"English words will flow out of it," said the sneering clerk.

Thus armed with the proper implements, Luís went to Amadeu's to test them. It requires a certain courage to display a notebook in a public place, unless you are a policeman or contractor, someone with a legitimate reason to pull one out of a pocket. Luís left his own in its brown paper wrapping for the duration of two fortifying copas and five SGs, until the café emptied of probable ridiculers. He slid it out of hiding and placed it in his lap. The pen proved an additional problem, so he took it to the W.C. Homens to fill. It was not immediately obvious to Luís how to get the ink inside. He pulled and twisted its various parts, peered inside the barren chamber and considered the viability of pouring, eye-dropping, smashing the fucking thing on the concrete floor.

The door opened as he considered this last option.

"Young da Silva. Boa tarde."

"Boa tarde, Montiego," he replied, quickly slipped the pen into his jacket pocket, and left.

His notebook rested on the chair, still not fully exposed to the cruel world. He put it back in its cover to carry to a safer place.

Montiego emerged from the toilet with something clasped inside his big hand. Luís felt his face redden and rose to leave.

"You left something in there," Montiego said and discreetly passed the bottle to Luís.

"Obrigado."

"Sit for a minute with me."

"I really can't. I'm late already."

"Sit!"

Luís folded himself down into the chair.

"What were you doing with a bottle of ink in the W.C. Homens? Don't tell me you are planning to give yourself a prison tattoo."

Luís laughed nervously. "There's an idea."

"I can have you brought in for questioning about subversive behaviour. It is not without suspicion to be writing secretly in the toilet."

"Don't make fun of me. I was trying to fill my pen. I wanted privacy."

"Your pen? May I see it?"

Luís handed the instrument over. Montiego felt its weight, rolled it appreciatively between his fingers like a fine cigar.

"Open that." He pointed to the ink bottle. While he dipped the nib, his fingers rotated the end of the pen one way and then the other.

"Nice one, that. You might wish to tighten it yourself. Not too hard, for it might not open again. I have a collection at home. I find a good pen helps me focus my thoughts and I use a different one for each type of writing: an antique for correspondence, a wide nib for strong business matters and a fine one for my bellas letras."

"You write?"

"My one secret pleasure. I am not as brave as you. I never do it publicly."

"What do you write about?"

"Nothing in particular. I just seem to ramble on. It is a noble pursuit, if futile. It gives me joy."

"I just had an idea it might be something I can do."

"Not can. Can is for the dime-store American novelists. You must want. You must need."

"You told me not so long ago those are mutually exclusive."

"Not in this instance." Montiego reached into his memory and easily called forth some of his favourite motivating words. "'Give me a song equal to the deeds of your so warlike people, a song destined to be known and sung throughout the world, if indeed a poet may achieve so much.'"

Luís laughed self-consciously. "I'm no poet."

"The literary world is large. There is room for many voices as long as they are true. Now, I shall leave you to become acquainted with your new friend."

Luís experienced thrill and terror as he once again pulled out the little notebook.

"I pretend to be a man of letters," it announced, inviting questions and contempt, and what if anyone should ever read it? If he lost it, to be found and critiqued by a real writer?

He considered worthy words to begin his endeavour.

"I want to write so that deathbed thoughts are of returning to this world as a Portuguese man. I need to write so I might learn to walk like a forcador in the ring, proud and fearless, through the rest of my life."

"Imagine the chicks," he thought, but left it off the page of nobler sentiments.

Montiego Makes His Second Mistake

"APRIL 1, 1974. My people have lost all faith in their institutions. Who can blame them? I believe they killed a man because their faith in me to uphold justice is gone. The example set for them for years by their own government. Dear God, what will become of our country if its most honest citizens resort to revenge and murder? It must end before we become an entire nation of murderers. I pray to you to show them the light, to return them to the peaceful, God-loving people they have always been."

Da Sousa read this sitting in Montiego's kitchen and snickered.

"You old woman, Montiego," he said out loud and put the journal in a paper bag found in the kitchen. He continued to ransack the house, looking for other damning articles, even though this was enough to have Montiego sent to the frying pans of Tarrafal prison.

The coup attempt had resulted in a doubling of the efforts of the secret police to ferret out subversives, and da Sousa had been instructed to investigate his colleague. All colleagues everywhere were being investigated. Caetano wasn't certain how far-reaching the plots against him might be, so he instructed no stone in a country paved with cobbles be unturned.

Da Sousa found some personal letters, uninteresting, but took them at any rate. He found ten notebooks, spanning twenty years of Montiego's noble if futile pursuit, and confiscated them also. The bits of paper upon which Montiego recorded the crimes of his country were stored in a large olive oil tin decorated with an unkind likeness of a forcador, one of eight young volunteers who step into the bull ring after the cavaleiro has performed his horseback artistry and face the stabbed and bleeding toiro barehanded, ultimately grabbing the bull by its horns, its neck or its tail.

"These will win favour," thought da Sousa. "Possibly even promotion." Here was a true enemy of the state, and he, Martino da Sousa, had sniffed him out. He dumped the contents into his bag and tossed the tin can across the room.

He waited for Montiego to return, only to see the look on his face when confronted with the chaos. He drank the man's wine, ate his food, and pissed on the floor for the simple satisfaction of it.

"The end is near for you, my friend," was all Montiego said when he finally arrived home.

Da Sousa, quite drunk by now, replied, "Not as near as yours," and passed out.

Montiego shook his head. "A special police force of stupid men. That is what they have built, and eight million people intimidated and beaten into submission, a nation of wretched morons who wander around to the tune of Fado, Fátima and football."

Still, he had to go somewhere until his world righted itself. He tied da Sousa's arms and legs and collected the things he needed.

Montiego was prepared. His bag had been carefully packed for months, hidden in the tool shed at the back of his house.

His final act was to warn Luís, for as a known friend, he was in danger of being questioned and, depending upon the depth of da Sousa's rage, imprisoned and tortured.

TWENTY-FOUR

Five-Hundred-Year-Old Truths

 "I HAVE HERE a letter from Montiego which he instructed me to read to you today as explanation for why he has disappeared. He has not fled in fear, but has gone to find a group which he believes at this very moment is making plans to restore our liberties and freedoms so we may once more become a nation of proud men. Do not breathe a word of what you hear tonight, for to do so will place everyone and everything in jeopardy and the shame will be on your shoulders if they fail."

Luís cleared his throat and in a grave tone affected for the occasion, began to speak Montiego's message.

"'My Friends. In times of great sadness and misfortune, I turn to Camões to remind me of the potential of this land of ours. Oh that I could find a muse of my own to give me the words to inspire your faith and courage.

Alas, Calliope is elusive and selective, so I must para-
phrase what she has already provided to another. I
expect Camões would not mind. I suspect he would be
grateful.

"'Is it possible that among Portuguese, with our
proud history, there can be found any who are unwilling
to make a stand for their land? It cannot be. Are we not
still the descendants of those who, under the banner of
the great Afonso Henriques, fought with such dash and
courage to overthrow the Spaniards?

"'We defined the word "bravery" time and time again:
the first to banish the Moors; the Spanish; on the fickle
seas and across the vast Alentejo plains. Look in the
dictionary under "fearless" and you will see the word
"Portuguese."

"'But a weak leader can sap the courage of a strong
people, and that is what we have here. My people are
not the people I see today, beaten into apathetic, fearful
men. My hope, my belief, lies in the wisdom that a
change of ruler will work a change in his people too.

"'Caetano, and Salazar before him, has allowed an
enemy to flourish at his gate while he has fought
another in a different part of the world, at the price of
depopulating and weakening this ancient kingdom and
squandering its most valuable resource: its people.
History has repeated itself and I believe we are in for
the most important challenge of our lives.

"'Have faith, my friends, that Venus once more is
looking down at her beloved Portuguese. She is weeping
for us, pitying us. Our beaches are drenched with her
tears and our mighty rivers grieve for the loss of our
courage and pride. As do I. As should you.

"'When the time comes, rise up with the liberators, though their shape may seem unlikely. Take up arms with them if necessary, and in the same spirit as the famed baker of Aljubarrota. Remember that she killed seven Castilian soldiers with just a wooden spoon, and baked them in her oven. Embrace them when they are the victors and bestow upon them that unshakeable loyalty and obedience which is the crowning quality of the Portuguese, the loyalty and obedience that has for too many years been misplaced. Find again the faith that enabled us to become the greatest country in the world, and will take us there once again. Do not waver or succumb to the promises of foolish men.

"'I will see you soon, my friends, and when I do I expect my glass to be kept full with the gift of Bacchus for many days and nights.

"'Rui Montiego.'"

Some in the room wept quietly. All were overcome with shame for their meek acceptance.

Luís raised his glass in a toast to better days.

"I hope everyone in this room will ready himself for the day when we are called upon to support the liberators. Prepare your shotguns and have them at the ready. I, for one, will be honoured to have the chance to fight to restore this country to its rightful state."

How Luisa Learns the Art of Trickery

JOSÉ RABELO LIVED and travelled in a modern caravan, a sleek and silvery Air Stream, bought from a stranded leftover hippie in Italy, fully equipped with a sink, miniature kerosene stove and toilet. While his riches included properties in Spain, France and Portugal, he chose not to live in any of them, preferring his caravan and a continual rental income. He claimed to have earned his fortune repairing tin works during the war, travelling through Europe with his tools and fixing pots and helmets, sharpening knives and bringing news to small towns. He did perform all these services, but the real money came from the aguardente he sold in gallon jugs. A few soldiers died from the toxic liquid, from poisoning or a stupid head the following day, but many people had fond memories of the funny little man who brought them temporary suicide.

He was sixty-five and never married, forever believing he would have an inclination later to take a wife. Of late, he had been so inclined, and could afford the prettiest, hard-working and preferably submissive Cigana he desired, and word quickly circulated throughout Europe that José Rabelo wished to see Ciganinhas, the younger the better, and virginal in both body and spirit, so Carminda Barbosa easily sent a message to him that she had a princess available for his scrutiny.

When Luisa saw him, she knew she could never survive a destiny with such a creature. It repulsed her to look at him and imagine his touch, his yellow fingernails, thick and slightly curved, scraping her skin. Hair grew out of all the places it might be interesting to kiss on another man — his ears and the tip of his nose — and his skin was scurfy under his thick white hair. He looked at her with mean and watery eyes, and smelled of cheap cologne.

She had no time to execute her salvation properly. One look at Luisa and he immediately agreed to the marriage, insisting to Carminda that the gift from her husband was too generous, and a bride price would be paid to ensure the woman's cooperation. He arranged to test her the following day, and since there was a great deal of money at stake Carminda placed the entire kumpania of one hundred Ciganos on guard. During the preparation of dinner, a feast in honour of their visitor, Luisa chose and meticulously scrubbed the largest carrot she could find and slipped it in the pocket of her skirt. All night she kept her hand there, feeling it, rubbing it; her saviour. She lay in bed that evening waiting for her mother's snoring to commence beside her. With only the slightest movement, she gently moved the vegetable between her legs, tickled herself for a few moments, then glided it in. An exertion of pressure at her target was necessary and she relished with spiteful pleasure the pain of the membrane tearing. She rocked a little back and forth, almost imperceptibly, and clenched her muscles around the hard, cool root. Unsure of what constituted loss of virginity, she continued to pump at it, and in the process discovered a surprisingly pleasant experience. The carrot grew warm inside her and she experimented at pushing it deeper. She twisted it and turned it, and finally rolled onto her belly. With the fingers of both hands active on other parts of her cona, she swallowed its entirety with a startling shudder.

Her mother stirred, muttered and rolled over. Luisa thought it best to leave the carrot inserted for the night to prevent the membrane from healing over, and soon fell asleep to dream of a real lover.

Da Sousa in Charge

 DA SOUSA STROKED the small soft head of Cãozinho as Paulo sat fidgeting in the chair opposite, slapping his leg for the dog to come to him for what little protection he might be able to provide. When the puppy made a movement towards his master, da Sousa roughly grabbed him by the scruff of his neck, causing a little yelp from both the dog and Paulo.

"Lovely dog, Paulo. I hope you keep him on a lead. He could so easily be crushed under the wheel of a car. Ever seen a dog flattened by a truck? Very sad. Very nasty. Keep him on a leash, son."

"I always do," he replied, keeping his eyes on Cãozinho. "But sometimes he just slips his head out of it."

Da Sousa nodded knowingly. "He is very small still.

See his little neck? Such a little, little neck. It could snap like a twig." He demonstrated this action for Paulo to ensure he understood. "But I didn't bring you here to talk about your dog. It's you I'm really curious about."

"What about me?"

"Why are you tormenting Senhora Brown?"

"Tormenting? I work for her."

Da Sousa rose from his chair to stand over Paulo.

"You are extorting money from her. You threatened to murder her animals. To eat them."

"Não!" cried Paulo. "I love the animals."

"Your friend Luís doesn't. He didn't tell you that?" Da Sousa shook his head, as though he felt pity, then slapped Paulo hard enough to knock him off his chair. The boy instinctively curled up in a ball.

"Get up," said da Sousa, kicking him. "Act like a man."

Paulo slowly rose to his feet without looking at da Sousa.

"Manny confessed, Paulo. He was in with Carlos, so I put him in jail for fraud. What I want to know now is how much money you received."

"No one received anything except Carlos. Manny gives all his money to Mama and she has none."

"Manny had plans to join Carlos in Germany, where they intended to make a new life together and leave your mother and you here to starve." Da Sousa shook his head in a faux forlorn manner. "It is very sad, actually."

"I don't believe it."

"I have his signed confession here for you to take to your mother. Perhaps now she will instruct that brother of hers to drop the case against Margaret Brown. If she does not, I will have to question you further, Paulo. Do you understand?"

Paulo nodded.

"I would hate to see anything happen to this little creature, Paulo. Keep him close to you."

Paulo knew da Sousa wasn't really talking about a truck, but he could not fathom why any person would want to harm his helpless little dog. He was afraid for his own safety and could only think of Luís as someone to help him.

By the time he arrived at Amadeu's he was not quite breathing, his lungs functioning only in tremors of sobs.

"Jesus, Paulo, what's wrong?" asked Luís, but his friend couldn't speak. He led him into the back storage room, away from mean eyes, and sat Paulo down on a wooden crate. "Wait here."

Luís went to the bar and got a shot of brandy, collected his own cerveja from the table where he had been sitting in guarded solitude, writing about princesses and gallant seamen.

"Drink this. All of it," he instructed.

Paulo did as he was told, and his body convulsed.

"Take a few deep breaths."

Gradually, it became easier to do so.

"Now, then, what can be so terrible, my friend?"

"Da Sousa. Manny's in jail. He threatened to kill Cãozinho." Tears returned and his voice stuck as he tried to breathe and speak at the same time. "He hurt me too."

"Is this about that woman?"

Paulo nodded. "Did you threaten to kill the animals, Luís?"

"Of course not! I threatened to set them free. They

would have starved to death without you taking care of them."

Paulo took more breaths.

"Where's Manny?" Luís asked.

"He didn't say exactly. Only that he's in a jail somewhere. He said he confessed and was in with Carlos."

"Have you told your mother?"

"Não. I came straight here."

"I need a drink. You want another?" Paulo nodded and Luís went and fetched a bottle.

"It helps me think," he said and drank a quick shot before pouring one for Paulo and a second for himself to set his brain straight. "Was Manny involved?"

Paulo stared at a detail of his shoe while he nodded. "He knew what Carlos had done and decided to wait until the house was almost finished."

"Fudis, Paulo! He can be legitimately arrested for that." Luís sighed. "How old is the bitch Margaret Brown?"

Paulo shrank a little at the harsh word. "I don't know. Sixty, maybe."

"Okay. Here's my idea. That place will one day be worth millions of escudos because people will realize this is the most beautiful place in the world. What if I tell her the money she paid may serve as a lease until she dies, or decides she misses the rain in England, at which time, ten years maybe, the property is yours. Then you can sell it for what it is truly worth. Everyone is happy."

Paulo agreed to try anything to make everyone happy.

For once in his life, Luís considered himself very clever indeed.

TWENTY-SEVEN

Montiego Joins the Captains

 DRESSED IN HIS old uniform, with medals and ribbons as testament to his loyalty and worth, Montiego entered the barracks in Lisboa. He was confident that this unlikeliest of havens was the safest place to avoid the persecutions of the secret police, that Spínola would persevere until his agenda was accomplished and that the failed coup was nothing more than a smokescreen to cover up a larger plan: the avant-garde troops sacrificed to lull Caetano and Tomás into a false sense of security while the main players carefully plotted the grand putsch.

"Ola, bom dia. I am looking for Major Otelo Saraiva de Carvalho. Is he available to see an old friend?"

"Your name, please?"

"Captain Luís vas de Camões." Had the attending officer been of a more fortunate family, he might have recognized the name of Portugal's most famous poet and quoted a few words to display his knowledge. The military, however, was filled with conscripts, illiterate, unskilled men with no option but to complete their four years' service, and mostly resigned to have any occupation at all.

"Wait here, please."

Montiego and de Carvalho had served together in Guinea-Bissau and passed the evenings reading aloud to one another, discussing better times and plans for the future. The two men were reunited the previous year when de Carvalho and his family spent the Easter weekend in the Algarve sunshine.

"You are still an honourable man, Montiego, and the G.N.R. is packed like sardines with dishonourable men. Be careful, and if you cannot keep your tongue silenced find me, I will arrange for safe passage to an easy position in Angola. The worst that can happen is you will be shot there. But you will not be tortured. We have not taught them that."

"Major de Carvalho is occupied and suggests you come again on Domingos at one o'clock, after church. He apologizes for any inconvenience."

"Obrigado. Bom dia."

Montiego realized his suspicions were accurate, that Otelo would have seen him, however briefly, if nothing was afoot, and he felt the adrenalin rush to his head. For the next two days he tried to relax, occupying himself with his favourite pleasures of the city. He walked through the gardens of São Jorge Castle and enjoyed the view of the Tejo from one of the parapets, bought luxury mustard seed sardines at the shop he knew of that sold nothing else, paused for a moment to study the tins lining its walls. He sat at a café and watched Lisboetas go about their day, tried to read their faces for anxiety, anticipation, apathy. His people were as they always were, pleasant, polite, animated as they talked of football, high prices, how the tourist season would be this year.

Saturday afternoon Lisboa shut down for the weekend, a civilized custom Montiego normally appreciated, but as the stores closed and the streets emptied, he felt sad and lonely, thinking of all the families enjoying an afternoon at the park. The presence of the D.G.S. seemed heightened in the absence of civilians, and he felt vulnerable, so he walked back up through the São Jorge area, where a lack of space forced people into the laneways to grill their lunch, catch up on gossip and visit with neighbours.

Domingos subway station was in the western suburb of Benfica, home to the football stadium, the former palace of the Marqueses de Fronteira and many luxurious quintas. Montiego scarcely recognized his friend out of uniform, but his own form was identifiable, not that it was unusual for men in Lisboa to be without legs, hands, feet. Otelo nodded as he walked by and Montiego followed at a distance. They crossed the street into the Parque Forestal Monsato, a large wooded area too hilly to be filled with casual Sunday strollers. Once they were well among the trees, Otelo stopped to light a cigar and allow his friend to catch up.

"So, Montiego, you understood. It's convenient during these times to have stations and days named the same. Have you come to join us?"

"It is time, Otelo. 'Give me the grand, resounding fury, not of rustic pipe or flute, but of the trump of war that fires men's breasts and brings a flush to the cheek.' Do you have a job for me?"

"We have many jobs and little time. It is good to see you, my friend."

Montiego established a secret headquarters in a farm-house in Santarem, forty-five miles northeast of Lisboa. A map of the capital covered one wall, with the crucial sites circled in red, arrows drawn to map the route of the liberators. Otelo came in the middle of the night and departed before dawn with notes and schedules. On three occasions, he brought other members of the organizing party, Major Vitor Alves, Captain Vasco Lourenço and Major Ernesto Melo Antunes, and together they wrote and reviewed the manifesto of the movement. Montiego received money, wine, food and names of possible conspirators to contact for civilian initiatives.

The officers agreed to Montiego's suggestion of sending a secret report to the British press, not revealing their plans but to give them a sense of the problems in the territories. In this way, they hoped to gain their sympathy for what they were about to do.

"Rhodesian troops are operating deep inside Portugal's African territory of Mozambique with orders to take no prisoners. There exists a close collaboration in the military field between Portuguese and Rhodesian troops, who include mercenaries from South Africa and other countries. Orders have been given by the Portuguese military command to 'mop up the land and kill any living soul.' There are massacres being committed and we are a group of officers outraged by such actions. We urge the media to report on these atrocities."

The thrill of subversion and danger was augmented by feeling rather like an excited bride, paying attention to all the details to ensure a perfect day. The components were similar to those of an elaborate wedding, with music and flowers and grand processions. While he was alone in the farmhouse, with *Os Lusiads* at his side as a constant source of inspiration, he dreamt up the poetic elements, the flourishes that would make the revolution the most memorable, and worthy of his country, his gentle people.

José Collects His Bride

LUISA LAY WAITING for him, naked and stiff and slightly drunk to help her through it. She couldn't look at him when he entered the tent, didn't want to see him at all so that the disgusting memory would have no visual aspect to it and might be more easily placed away. Her eyes were closed against him and she hoped he would not make any noise either, leaving only the senses of smell and touch to forget.

He pulled off the sheet covering her so he could admire his future property while he undressed. The early evening air was cool and Luisa felt her nipples pop out from their golden aureolae.

"Ahhh," he whispered. "Just as the mare beats the road, so the young bride wants the penis." He reached down and roughly pinched her successively on each breast, lingering on the second nipple while it hardened involuntarily between his fingers. "Mmmmm. You will please me, Luisa."

Her prayers were answered, for he was in such a rush, was so consumed with desire for her young, ripening body, that she barely had time to consider how a penis felt in her canal. He heaved at her exactly six times and collapsed, making Luisa think of an ass, and she giggled. He caught his breath and rolled over, dressed and instructed her to hurry with the sheet.

Roma custom is for the potential bride to present the blood-stained sheet for examination and verification, plum wine sprinkled on the area to cause virginal blood to spread into the shape of a flower. Failure to do so meant the bride was not pure, and if the man still wished to marry her, a lower price may be demanded of her parents. A successful sheet was paraded through the town or camp by two chosen virgins, and the wedding celebrations began. Couples often tried to remedy an unsuccessful sheet with a few drops of pig's blood, most commonly as a result of the groom's failure, not the bride's past.

José waited outside with Carminda while the chosen member of the Kris performed the ritual. Now that the time was before him, José's impatience to be married manifested itself in a steady state of semi-arousal. When he thought of possessing such a beautiful nubile body, of the things he would spend the rest of his life doing to her, he regretted that his life was drawing to a close and determined to spend every day pursuing pleasurable amusements with this girl.

"She is impure," the judge announced, emerging from the tent. "She admitted it."

"Não!" shouted José, and turned to Carminda. He slapped her hard so that she reeled, then pushed the man aside and entered the tent where Luisa was dressing.

"Puta! You like cock, do you?" He didn't even bother to remove his pants, just the belt, which he used to secure her arms behind her, and pulled his penis through the fly.

Luisa was prepared for this and accepted it as a fair exchange for escaping years with the man. His rage was such a powerful stimulant, and he was getting on in years, that the torture didn't last long. When he finished, he wept over his loss, spat on her cona to curse it with fruitlessness, and left. She could hear her mother trying to negotiate.

"She is still a beautiful girl. You enjoyed her body, Não?"

Luisa lifted the flap at the back of the tent and rolled out. On her hands and knees, she crawled slowly until she felt she had enough of a lead to stand and run.

TWENTY-NINE

Why the Gypsies
Know Everything

 SHE STOPPED ONCE to assess the danger and felt the sea's pull in a vertiginous moment, so didn't look again. Waves reached up to the narrow pathway, the spray and the rain making it slippery and perilous. One great swell and she would be sucked into its crest, held suspended for a moment, a pause long enough to consider her fate: to be hurled like common debris against the rocks. She didn't know if her hiding spot would be safe from the ire of this sea, but could think of no other place to go. Her mind spun in confusion and refused to straighten itself out to determine the status of the tide. All that it could focus on was the mechanical motion of each footstep being firmly planted before the next. Her progress was slow as a result, and at times she feared she had stupidly missed the turn to the cave, or that it was no longer there but crumpled into itself from the rain. She hugged the sandy wall and tried not to notice that there was nothing on its surface to cling to.

At last she recognized the entrance and relief slowed the beating of her heart. A light flickered inside and it was a welcoming sight, not frightening, for nothing in her imagination could be worse to endure than the events of that evening.

"Olá, boa noite," she called out and heard some scuffling in the dirt before two raggedy young men appeared in the big hole, unwashed and shabbier than the poorest Rom. They stared at Luisa for a moment, assessed why a Cigana would be on the side of a cliff in the middle of a rain storm, looked in vain at one another for the answer.

"What do you want?"

"I need shelter from the storm. I am in danger and need to hide here tonight. I did not know it was occupied."

"Go away. There is not enough room for three."

"I have aguardente, which I will share with you. I will entertain you with stories to make the night pass more pleasantly. I will even allow you to use my body if you wish. Please. My life is at risk, and I cannot walk that path in the approaching darkness."

The two men smiled, scarcely believing their good fortune. A drink of aguardente would have been enough to allow the girl to stay and they both thought her quite stupid for offering so much more.

"Okay. For one night. Come in."

"Obrigada."

She stepped into the hole and was surprised at the

amount of heat generated from the fire. Its flames threw dancing shadows on the walls and she felt relief and contentment replace the tension in her body. She opened her bag and extracted a small bottle.

"Here is the aguardente, as promised. Be careful with it. It is not like your Portuguese brandy and you may not be accustomed to its power."

"Bah! Listen to the Cigana. The Portuguese make the finest aguardente. You will see who cannot handle it."

Luisa nodded. "I must remove my wet clothes to allow them to dry properly. Do either of you have an extra shirt I might wear?"

"That depends. Do we get to watch you undress?"

"Not yet. Later, when I have been warmed by the fire, I will dance for you. After that, I will undress for you. I am shy and require the alcohol."

The men looked at one another again, shrugged. They had all evening.

"I am Christophe, and he is Vasco. Here, you may wear this." He gave her a garish shirt with wide lapels and several missing buttons. She moved to the darkest corner of the cave and stripped off her soaking skirt and blouse. Her undergarment, a pair of terrycloth short shorts, suited the fashionable shirt, and lent her a stylish persona. Polyester had not touched her skin before and it brushed her bare nipples to attention. The moment she stood back in the light, the two men were suddenly afraid of her, shy and uncomfortable, for she was no longer an object of derision, but a beautiful woman, and clearly their superior.

"Now then, give me a drink and I shall tell you a story. It is about a cave and a Gypsy as well, so listen up. There are always meanings for coincidences such as this."

Christophe passed her the bottle and she took two small sips before passing it on to Vasco and then sat cross-legged across from them and the fire so the flames could flicker in her eyes to mesmerize them.

"Once upon a time, in the olden days, Gypsy caravans travelled from village to village, city to city, and my people would beg and tell fortunes for a piece of bread."

"Olden days?" Vasco laughed. "What about now?"

"Please," she said indignantly. "I am trying to tell the story as it has been told to me. In some countries, Gypsies must live in houses because the law forbids them to move around. This story comes from such a place, so it is about better times, not the present."

Vasco smirked and nudged Christophe. Luisa shook her head at their childishness, rolled her eyes in good humour.

"So, the Gypsies wandered from place to place. In one city there was a woman who didn't like her neighbour — the two women always quarrelled, day after day, from having to live beside one another their whole lives. One day, this woman asked a Gypsy girl to tell her fortune: 'Come here,' she called out. 'I'll give you whatever you want if you can tell me what is in my heart.'

"Just at that moment, the neighbour came out of her house and made an insulting gesture at the first woman. The Gypsy girl noticed this and said: 'You live in a really bad neighbourhood and things are not going well for you in this house. Your neighbours are jealous of you because you are smart and a good housewife.'

"'Bravo!' the woman replied. 'You found out everything. What do you want me to give you? I'd even give you my heart.' So she gave the girl bread, cheese and money, and as the Gypsy was about to leave for her camp the woman said to her: 'Come tomorrow. I have something for you to do.' And the Gypsy promised to return.

"Now, since Gypsies were forbidden to camp for the night near the city, they had set up their tents some distance away. The next day, as the Gypsy girl walked back to the city, all of a sudden it started to rain very hard, harder even than it does on this day. It was the month of March, a March as mean and wet as the one just passed. The Gypsy girl searched everywhere for shelter and finally found an entrance to a cave, much bigger than this. She went inside and looked around carefully in the depths, where she saw a small light. As she got closer, she saw it was a large fire and thought she'd warm up nicely there.

"From the shadows near the fire, not two, but twelve young men in nice clothes and good shoes came forward and said to her all at the same time so that it was like a group singing: 'Welcome. Tell us, little girl, where are you going?'

"'I'm on my way back to the city, but I got caught in the downpour, and what could I do? I found this cave and came in through the entrance and found your fire.'

"'Do you know why it's raining?' they asked. 'It's the month of March — and in March the cold is awful and it rains all the time. What a terrible month it is!'

"'Don't say that!' she answered. 'The month of March is the best.'

"'Why?'

"'Because it brings us April, when spring comes. Without the month of March, we wouldn't have any spring. And if there were no February, there would be no March.'

"And so for each of the months she had something good to say.

"'And now where are you going?' they asked her.

"'I want to return to the city to earn enough money so that my family may eat tonight.'

"'Bring your sack over here,' they said, and filled it and sewed it up. 'Take this, but don't open it until you get home.'

"The girl returned to her camp and her mother and father were very angry with her for not going to the city.

"'Please don't be angry,' she said to them. 'I didn't go to the city but I found twelve handsome young men and they gave me this — what it has inside, I don't know.'

"They opened it and what did they find? All golden coins, for the twelve young men were really the twelve months and the Gypsy girl, because she hadn't insulted any of the months, got the treasure.

"The next day, the weather was perfectly clear. The Gypsy girl ran to the woman she had promised to see the previous day. As much gold as she'd gotten, she still wanted to beg, for that is the Gypsy way, and why people say we are never satisfied.

"On the way, the girl met the quarrelsome neighbour, who recognized her and said: 'Whatever she gives you, I'll give you more. Now tell me what you want.'

"'What can I say?' she replied. 'I don't want you to give me anything, for God has provided.'

"'What did God give you?'

"She told the woman how she'd found the cave and gone in to get out of the rain.

"'Where's the entrance to this cave? I'll go and see for myself.'

"So the quarrelsome neighbour went on her way to the twelve months, but without knowing who they were. She found the entrance just where the Gypsy girl had told her it was, and went into the cave, pretending to be cold.

"'What month is it, old woman, that it is so cold outside?' asked the twelve months.

"'It is March — the cruellest, worst month in the year.'

"'What do you have to say about February?'

"'That stupid February?' and she went on to curse all the months, without a good word to say about any of them: July was so hot you couldn't move; August was responsible for bringing insects; September made the leaves fall from the trees, and so on.

"'Give us your sack.' They filled it and sewed it up and told her to open it only when she got home. She hoped to find gold inside — it was heavy — and she thought it would be the same as the Gypsy's. But when she got back to the city and opened it, what was inside? Lots of snakes that came out and ate everything in sight, including her!

"Her neighbour said, 'The Gypsy knew everything. My neighbour was truly a bad woman, so the Gypsy did her magic.'

"And that is why since then, people, even today, still say Gypsies know everything, and it's true. They lived well in those days, and we live even better today."

The men laughed at her.

"Such as now?" said Christophe. "Hiding here in a cave? That is living well, is it?"

"It is better than being stuck with a mean neighbour to torment you every day of your life."

"And you are running from such a problem?"

"A bigger problem even than that! My mother and father made a marriage match for me that I did not want, so I tricked them all and ran away. I have brought shame to my family and deprived them of riches, as he had a great amount of wealth. For that, I believe my mother would like to kill me. Pass the bottle, please, all this talk has made me thirsty."

It was now half empty. Vasco, she noticed, leaned heavily on one elbow to keep himself upright. Christophe seemed more lucid, so she returned the bottle to him.

"Gypsies don't know everything. It was only common sense. Any idiota could have figured it out about the neighbour."

"Exactly. That is the point, but common sense is essential, não? Not everyone uses it."

"I suppose."

"I have told a story so it is your turn. You know why I am in this cave, but I do not know why you are, and certainly that is a more interesting story."

"It is boring. We are running to Spain to escape the army, like so many others."

"And what will you find in Spain?"

"I do not know."

"We are not so different, then."

He thought for a moment whether to be insulted by this comparison.

"Não, we are not. It is still our cave, however, and I think now I would like to see you dance."

He reclined against the wall in a position of kingly observance, with his hands clasped behind his head to keep it aloft.

Luisa didn't require music, for the wind and the storm and the sea provided that. She closed her eyes and simply let her body become a part of it, and even though it was the most seductive dance, they were too drunk to respond and fell asleep, hypnotized by the rain falling in her hips.

She made a little pillow of her slip and pulled her skirt over her for a blanket. Just before she fell asleep, she added a footnote to her folktale and smiled contentedly.

"And that is how the Gypsy princess came to trick three men in one day and why to this day, they must always use trickery."

THIRTY

A Princess Tale

 EVEN FROM A DISTANCE of several hundred yards, she knew the small shape on the sand belonged to him, had intuitively known he would be there even before the final turn of the cliff before the beach. She wanted to run to him and fling herself into his arms, to be held and protected forever, but it was not her nature to do so. Instead, she paused to allow him the opportunity, and followed his line of vision, for he stared at something on the horizon. She saw nothing but the sun making a sudden appearance in the distance. He sensed her presence in the quiet and turned his head. Being of a different nature entirely, he ran to her and threw his arms around her to hold her tightly.

"When the sun shone down at me, I knew it was you who brought it."

He released her just enough to witness her entire being.

"Look at you, all dressed in your Cigana princess clothes. You are gorgeous."

She laughed. "They are my wedding clothes."

Luís recoiled.

"Oh, but I did not get married!" she added. "I couldn't. I've run away, Luís, and spent the night in the cave back there."

"Meu Deus! Are you all right?"

"Sim. I'm fine. I am dirty and desperately need to bathe, hungry and thirsty and tired, but I am not the wife of José Rabelo and that is all that matters."

"Come, let me hold you once more, to know this is real." He embraced her again but with tenderness instead of passion, stroked her head and softly kissed its crown. Luisa had never been held like this, had not experienced the luxurious warmth of such loving compassion, and felt she would cry.

She pulled away. "I need to think," she said. "I need somewhere safe to stay for a little while."

"I have a place. It is safe. Are you all right by yourself here for an hour or so while I make things ready?"

"Yes, I think so. I can always escape into the sea if they come for me here. No one in my family can swim but me. If I am not here when you return, I will meet you inside the cemetery. They won't go there."

"I am so happy, Luisa. Don't worry. I will take care of everything."

His house stood shrouded by the tallest cypress and palm trees so that most people forgot its existence. As the wind blew, its windows became eyes peeking out at the world through fingers of fronds and slender branches. The surrounding fields were on fire with spring poppies, and bamboo groves created a natural barrier to intruders unaware of the pathway. He moved from room to room, noted what was required, but mostly it was perfect, as always. He entered the lush and overgrown garden and once again sensed something magical about this space with its wild roses and cacti living in harmony, creeping succulents sprawling lazily in fuchsia bloom across the stones of the courtyard. The poppies had found their way inside as well, and seemed to live up to their name between the cracks. They would dine here this evening, he thought, under the stars and with the wind in the trees as their company, the sound of the sea joining from a distance.

People sometimes came in the summer, but never earlier than June, and they did not make themselves known to the villagers. He had repeatedly asked the shopkeepers, wine merchants and restaurant owners, and no one remembered anything about the owners. Sometimes he imagined they must be ghosts and that the house itself existed only in the spirit world, but there it was, slightly dank and musty from black mould growing on the damp walls. Every house had the mould that year, and Luís had made some good money whitewashing with a broom. He wiped the worst walls with bleach and cleaned only the rooms they would need, made up the biggest bed with fresh linen expropriated from his mother's clothesline. In the kitchen, he unpacked freshly baked pão, goat cheese, vinho, avocados and sardines, and placed a bunch of wild freesia in a vase on the table. He surveyed the house once more to ensure it would be comforting to her, and went to collect the one missing object.

He blindfolded her once they reached the cemetery and led her gently by the hand.

"Imagine that I am taking you to another place entirely, where no one can hurt you and nothing but love and passion and joy exist. You must breathe through your lovely little nose and you will smell freedom in the air."

"What is it?"

"You can smell it?"

"Sim."

"'I know a bank whereon the wild thyme blows, where oxlips and the nodding poppy grows. There sleeps Titania some time of the night, lull'd in these flowers with dances and delight.' I would like to tell you I wrote that verse for you, but I cannot disgrace the honourable William Shakespeare in such a way. It is believed that the thyme which is all around us now is beloved by fairies and so they will protect us. They live in the house I am taking you to, I am certain of it, for it is magical and filled with a special sense. I can't explain it otherwise. One day, I will own it according to the law, but for the moment, I own it only in spirit. It is my home as much as any place will ever be, and I think you will feel it also. We are almost there."

"Whose house is it?"

"I do not know. People come for a month each year.

I think they are French because they have the most wonderful taste."

"Are you certain you are not part Cigano, perhaps?"

"Perhaps I am, or perhaps I was in a previous life and still have some of your ways about me."

"Another life? You believe that?"

"Sometimes, yes. Don't you? I thought your people are of Indian descent and therefore Hindi."

"I don't know anything but that I am Rom and that my people are on a pilgrimage of repentance for turning away Mary and Joseph when they needed shelter to birth the baby Jesus."

"For how many thousands of years must you repent?"

"Until we are forgiven and accepted. We have an expression which speaks to the situation when we talk about death: 'Bury me standing. I've been on my knees too long.'"

He stopped and hugged her to him. "You may get off your knees if you wish to now."

When he finally removed her blindfold, she believed she had stepped into a fairy tale of a real princess. The house was indeed secluded from the rest of the world, not only in the physical sense but on a sensual level as well, its peacefulness a narcotic. They did not speak, for the sound would ruin the spell, and moved slowly indoors, through each room until they arrived at the bedroom on the top floor with a view of the sea.

They stood at the window to be further blessed by the beauty and the soft breeze. Luís was behind her and slowly caressed the miracle before him. He felt he must touch every inch of her, beginning with her face, to know it all by this other sense, for sight was not enough; he had to experience her with all his senses. His fingertips moved along her neck, long and thin, but not fragile, across shoulders as smooth as marble, down arms and fingers. He felt her waist flare slightly into hips, boyish in their slenderness, but with the promise of the full power of a woman. He was afraid to touch her breasts, unsure of his ability to control himself after that, but Luisa took his hands and placed them there herself, sighing quietly, surprised. He breathed deeply, turned her gently to face him. He kissed her eyelids, her earlobes, brushed his lips against hers, tasted. Salty and sweet. He undid the buttons of her blouse and slipped it off her shoulders to reveal a slip of sheer muslin. The skirt she undid herself and he picked her up and placed her on the bed, kissed her gently on the forehead.

"Go to sleep, my princess."

Luisa's mouth quivered. "Have I displeased you somehow?"

"Shhh. Querida Luisa. You are perfection. I only wish to wait until you are feeling better."

When she awoke, a dusky light filled the room, and Luís sat in a chair by the bed watching her.

"So this is not a dream or is it?" she asked in a whisper.

"It is the most fantastic dream from which you never need awake."

"I must tell you something, Luís, or I will forever feel I have tricked you, robbed you of your beautiful moments."

"Nothing you tell me can do that."

"I am not pure. In my heart, yes, but not my body."

He considered this.

"Your heart is what matters."

"You will still be my first lover, for the memory of what happened is already faded. I made certain of that. You are a new and beautiful experience, but I had to tell you so you wouldn't believe I cheated or tricked you."

The magnitude of what had happened, the consequences, rose to the surface of her youthful consciousness. Tears rolled down Luisa's face as she confessed her shame, opened up her fear that he'd cast her away.

He wiped away the moistness with the edge of the sheet.

"You are not allowed to be sad in this house. It will stay in the walls and infect everyone who enters. My beautiful Cigana's eyes will be swollen and red. Come, the sunset has painted the sky an incredible shade of orange tonight. We shall toast its contribution to the perfect day and welcome the moon, which is full and will provide the most beautiful light for our celebrations."

Candles illuminated the palms, the geraniums in pots, and spread strange shadows. They danced in the breeze to soft music from a transistor radio.

"Is this how all gadje live?" she asked him.

"Não, but we can. It is only the beginning if you wish it to be so."

For an entire week, they lived wrapped in the magic of the house, leaving only to walk to the secret beach to bathe and make love again. Luís went into the village to get food and cooked for her, always using the rosemary and thyme and other wild herbs he described

185

in mythical verse to her. He found wonder in everything and knew this was the nature of love.

"So what do you think?" he finally asked her. "Would you like this to be your life?"

"It is the life of a dream."

"Sim. So what about my destiny? Would you like to reconsider my palm now?"

"I lied. I made it all up. I cannot read palms or tell fortunes at all. Please don't be angry with me. I did it only to make you feel better."

"I know. I don't believe in fortune tellers."

"I promise I will never lie to you again, Luís. I don't like lying, one reason I ran away. My whole life has been a lie because I wasn't certain I wanted to be a Gypsy. We are free in many ways, but I have not been free within my self, within my own life. It shouldn't be important, according to our beliefs, but it is to me."

"Do you feel free here?"

"Yes, even though we are in a way imprisoned here. Inside I do."

Amalia Rodrigues, the famous fadista, sang about lost love on the radio.

"She has the voice of an angel, don't you think?" he asked her.

"I never thought angels were sad."

"They must be, for they are dead and away from their homes and the people they love."

"But they are in heaven. Surely heaven is better than earth. Isn't that why we all hope to get there?"

"Perhaps it is just that we do not want the alternative."

"Your music is so sad. Why is that? I still don't understand what has been your great suffering."

"It is Fado, which comes from the Latin for fate. Any misfortune or unhappiness we attribute to fate, so it is sung in Fado. We long for a happiness that always eludes us, that our destiny has snatched away."

"But surely you can do something about it. Our music is filled with passion and lust for life and we have been oppressed, hated and feared for hundreds of years."

"I am doing something about it now. I did not allow fate to snatch you away."

"Perhaps you were correct the first day we met and this is the result."

"How is it that you are so young and yet so wise? You make me feel foolish."

"I am a Gypsy, and when we sing we sing about how Gypsies know everything."

"So what do you know about me? Like about me?"

"I know that you are shy and uncertain about yourself, and I like that, it makes me feel strong. Your touch is as though you are handling the most precious thing in the world and your smell is the sea and the earth, without horrid cologne. I like your eyes, the way they take me inside of you. Most of all, I like your spirit. You have an innocence not found in my people, which allows you to find beauty in the smallest gifts the world has to offer. It is appealing to me, and I want it for myself. Now, you tell me."

"I don't think I know anything about you, really."

"What you like is what you know."

"Okay. The way you move, it is like a symphony being performed by the finest musicians. Your touch is like fire. Your confidence and spirit and pride make me want to have them for myself, they inspire me to it. You are perfection to me, gorgeous and gorgeousity. Your smile can light the sky in the dead of night and your eyes frighten me for what they can see. Sometimes, in your eyes, I see you know me better than I know myself. I think I must have known you before, in another life. I wish to wake up to your smile every day for the rest of my life. That I know with all my heart."

"And what if my Gypsy blood causes me to be discontent with one place, settled, sleeping in a bed and enclosed in your walls?"

"Then we will take a blanket down to the beach and sleep beneath the stars."

"And if I wish to dance the flamenco, how will you react?"

"I will watch in admiration and awe."

"If I wish to be with another man?"

"I will kill him."

"Very passionate. We have no word for envy in our language. It is not necessary."

"I wish to marry you, Luisa. Please say yes."

THIRTY-ONE

The Lisboa Road

"BUT HOW WILL I GET to Quinta dos Angelicus to feed the animals?" said Paulo.

"You may have the van during my absence," Luís told him. "You can earn extra money making the deliveries, and use it to transport new animals. It really is more practical than having them follow you all the way out there."

Paulo liked the procession; practical was not important.

"Why don't you take the van?"

"I can't be driving around Lisboa in a bullfighting van. Besides, it uses too much petrol and I'm not certain it would make it all the way there. Come on, be a pal."

Paulo chewed at a bit of tough skin around his fingernail, not knowing how to say no, and Luís recognized and pushed through this window of opportunity.

"I will do anything you want in return, Paulo. Just name it."

He screwed up his face so that it appeared contorted from the effort of thinking.

"Will you teach me to read and write?"

"Piece of cake. No problemo. We'll start as soon as I return."

"Okay, then. How long will you be?"

"A week at most. I can't afford to not work for longer than that."

They shook hands and exchanged keys.

"You're a good friend, Paulo. I won't forget it."

Paulo grinned broadly.

For Luís, the experience of driving a motorbike with a girl displayed on the back surpassed his finest fantasies, better even than the previous week of finally discarding his virginity. This sensation comprised pride and a deep comfort, like a heavy pile of wool blankets on a cold and stormy night, exciting, but settled, and more real. He pushed the motorcycle to go as fast as possible to force Luisa to hold him tighter, and thought of driving down the Avenida da Liberdade with Luisa's hair flying like a banner, her arms around him and the whole of Lisboa as their witness. The combination of the vibration of the bike, inquisitive hands all the while exploring new places on his chest, and her frequent shifts forward against his lower back had contributed to an uncomfortable hardness for the past several miles.

They stopped after an hour to stretch, drank a fast cerveja and relieved their mutual longing against the back of the cantina. Luisa was as insatiable as Luís, and after experiencing the intense pleasure of potentially public and therefore necessarily hasty sex had him stop at regular intervals on various pretences. Their journey was slowed considerably as a result, and Luís was grateful, for he didn't much want to meet her father, didn't know what he would say to the man, and was afraid he would deny them their happiness together. He would prefer to drive straight through Lisboa and continue to the wild north of the country, where the Douro flows between deep valleys of ancient grape vines. There they would have their honeymoon, camped under the stars and planning for the future.

The rain began just outside Grândola, forcing them to detour into the little town to find a sheltering pensione. It was not a coastal rain that would stop after an initial downpour, so they sat by a window in a makeshift café and drank the patron's homemade vinho verde while they stared into each other's eyes and entwined fingers in varying formations. At half past midnight, a plaintive and beautiful song played on the transistor radio they brought with them for such occasions.

"Listen, he is singing about this place. 'Grândola, dusky town, land of brotherhood: it is the people who hold sway within your walls.' It is another sign, Querida."

"What is this sign?"

"That we are doing what is right, we have made the correct decision and life is changing for us, moving in a good direction."

"I do not need a sign to know that. It is all around my heart."

Montiego had recruited a subversive disc jockey to lay down the soundtrack to the day's events, and in a lapse of discretion resulting from his immeasurable pride over the role the rebel concluded the song with a deviant identification of the national radio program.

"Vila Morena, by José Zeca Afonso, coming at you from studio mad cow."

"Merda," said Montiego, pacing outside the little booth. "Don't be clever."

"Grândola, Vila Morena" was in fact the secret signal to the troops to proceed. Less than two hours earlier the countdown had begun with "And After the Farewells" and two hundred junior officers went on alert. The call had come in from Otelo to give the go-ahead, and by 3 a.m. the rebel soldiers were in command of the vital points of Lisboa, welcomed by tired, frustrated workers with vigorous embraces. No force was necessary to assume control of the train station, the airport, the subway; the lifelines to a successful operation were handed over with relief and childish joy. The larger challenge lay in coaxing the people to go home quietly until the threat of resistance passed. Not a single man agreed to forgo participation, so they were instructed to act as foils, to carry on as though nothing were amiss.

The young lovers slept off the vinho in a room next to the patron and his wife. When Luís awoke at five with a miraculous and unprecedented erection, he felt compelled to share his good fortune with Luisa. They made love quickly in the squeaky bed, which made them both giggle uncontrollably, then entered the still-dark morning.

By the time they arrived in the capital, the sun was rising, its clear light filtering through the cracks between the new highrise buildings leading into the city. Lisboa is not a morning city, so the streets belonged to them, and Luís zig-zagged across the lanes. It was not until they approached the massive statue of the Marquis de Pombal overlooking the lower city that particular dictator had designed, that the presence of tanks became known to them. A cordon of vehicles blocked access to the wide Avenida da Liberdade and soldiers casually waved motorists away from following the tanks.

"Meu Deus, Querida, is there a festa? A parade? Or is it really happening?"

"Who are they?"

"I suspect they are the liberators, successful this time in reaching Lisboa, but I can't be certain. I know where we can go to watch, where we will be safe in case there is any trouble."

He drove them up a succession of narrow, winding lanes to the top of the Bairro Alto. Luís helped Luisa climb up and over the six-foot wall in the section he knew of with footholds and followed her into the lush vegetation of the botanical gardens.

"Come. I will show you my favourite tree. It is perfect to climb and provides the best view of the avenida."

They ran through the misty park because Luís didn't wish to miss a moment of the spectacle. They climbed into the upper branches of an old oak tree, a gift to the gardens from Canada.

"Give me the radio," he said to her and she pulled it out of her bag. He turned it on and twisted the dial until he got a clear signal. After a few final bars of a banned song, there was a pause, and then a familiar voice.

"This is the Movement of the Armed Forces. We are, at this time, calling on all army and police forces to avoid any dangerous clashes. There is no deliberate intention to shed blood unnecessarily, but that will happen in the case of any provocation. We appeal to all soldiers and police without other instructions to return to their barracks and await the orders that will be given here by the Armed Forces Movement. All commanders that attempt by any means to force their subordinates to fight against the movement will be held severely responsible. We are attempting to liberate the country from the present government. Please await further instructions. Viva Portugal."

"Viva Portugal! Did you hear that, Querida? It was my friend Montiego's voice, I am sure. He told me there was a group within the armed forces who were planning a coup and that he was going to join them. If it is, they won't hurt the people, they are not interested in that, only in stopping the wars in the colonies."

"But what about the rest of the army?"

"That's the danger, but I think most will join the movement now. It's only the old generals and the D.G.S. who may cause trouble, I think. We'll wait here to see if any come, and if not we'll go and celebrate in the street."

They remained riveted in their tree awaiting additional reports from the radio. The broadcasts increasingly mimicked a commentary of a football match and diminished as news reportage, which caused Luís to smile at Montiego's sense of irony.

"Three waves of the supposedly loyal Seventh Cavalry Regiment were sent against the liberating officers positioned in the Praça do Comércio. The first wave immediately went over to the rebels, and the second also joined after its commander was arrested. The final group, led by a brigadier general, fought for a few minutes in a vain attempt and then broke off, undecided and wavering. We remind the people, at this time, to remain indoors to avoid any bloodshed. Viva Portugal."

Lisboetas ignored the unreasonable plea. As they slowly awoke to the news of a coup, they filtered out of their houses to witness the spectacular event. By ten, the wide street named for the republican victory against the monarchy sixty-five years earlier was lined with people cheering on the soldiers.

"I think we can safely go down there," Luís said.

"I'm trusting you, Luís, but please, don't let go of my hand. I would hate to lose you in all those people. I don't know what would happen to me."

He kissed her for providing an opportunity to protect her. "I would not risk losing you, even for the exhilaration of participating in our liberation."

They walked quickly down the twisting street and came out on the Avenida da Liberdade at the same time that several platoons of troops arrived on foot and formed lines along the sidewalks. Once the final soldier took his position, all raised their carbines ceremoniously and concurrently and placed a red carnation in the end.

A musical roar rose from the crowd, sounding finally like a song of salvation rather than unkind fate. Luís couldn't keep the tears from his eyes, and he stood and sobbed. His neighbour in line, a portly old woman, hugged him to an ample bosom and her son grabbed Luisa, picked her up and kissed her fully on the mouth before setting her back down. He handed her a bottle of wine, stolen from the broken display window of a shop during the early hours of the coup, and she gratefully took a drink. Many citizens had wine and they passed the bottles to the soldiers before bestowing kisses on their smiling faces.

Luisa joined the celebrations listlessly.

"What do you think will happen to the prisoners in the jails?" she finally asked Luís.

"Querida! I'm so sorry. Not only have I let go of your hand, I have ignored your worries. Come, we'll try to get over there."

He took her hand and pushed through the throngs. Slowly, they made their way back to where the motorcycle was parked.

A large crowd had already formed outside Caxias prison, singing patriotic songs and awaiting announcements from officials on the status of the political prisoners inside.

"They will be released, of course," said a man Luís's age. "It is only a question of timing and organization. They don't want to release the real criminals in error."

Luís turned to Luisa. "What was your father's crime?"

"What is my crime? He is a Cigano. He had no documents."

"That's it? You're sure he didn't steal something, perhaps?"

"Please, Luís. My father didn't need to steal."

"Forgive me. I sometimes forget they needed no

reason. Nothing seems to be happening here, though, and I doubt it's the immediate priority to release prisoners. We'll go to the barracks to hear news directly. Maybe even Spínola will show up."

Several thousand people had had the same idea, were gathered outside the building where Premier Caetano hid, and they shouted angrily for the assassin to show himself. When General Spínola arrived, they chanted his name, and he smiled broadly while waving his riding crop at his people. Premier Caetano had summoned Spínola, had requested he be allowed to hand over his power to the general "so that the government would not fall in the streets," but in truth he would discuss surrender only with a person of suitable stature.

"I am not the leader of this movement," announced Spínola to the crowd. "I did not act against the government, but if it has the good sense to find a solution, I think I will be doing a service by speaking to the rebels on their behalf." Spínola went inside the building and a group of uniformed sailors formed a line across the front. A bugler played the Portuguese national anthem and began a march down the street, others falling smartly in behind.

This was Montiego's final official role in the events and he summoned the crowd to join them in a celebratory parade through the city. They marched, fifty abreast, drawing the people away from the more volatile locations with shouts of "Victoria!" and "Viva Portugal!" In the Plaza Dom Pedro IV, a waiting officer took over and reminded the people of the intended gentle nature of the revolution. Montiego circulated through the crowd to distribute carnations from an enormous bundle carried by a young soldier, and if his hand was not shaken it was because a bottle of vinho had been thrust in it instead.

La Liberdade

 "CONSIDERING THAT AFTER thirteen years of fighting overseas, the present political system has been unable to define an overseas policy leading to peace among Portuguese of all races and creeds;

"Considering the growing climate of total detachment of the Portuguese in relation to political responsibilities they owe as citizens, the growing development of a situation of constant appeals to duty with a parallel denial of rights;

"Considering the necessity to clean up institutions, eliminating from our system of life the illegal acts that the abuse of power has legalized;

"Considering, finally, the duty of the armed forces and the defence of the nation, signifying also the civic liberty of its citizens;

"The Movement of the Armed Forces, which has just achieved the most important civic mission in recent years, proclaims to the nation its intention of completing a program of salvation for the country and the restitution to the Portuguese people of the civil liberties of which they have been deprived.

"To effect this, the government will be handed over to a junta of national salvation, which will carry out the lines of the Armed Forces Movement plan, whose details will be given to the nation later.

"As soon as possible there will be general elections for a constituent national assembly, whose powers, by its representation and free election, will permit the nation to choose freely its own form of social and political life.

"In the certainty that the nation is with us, supporting our aims, and will accept with good grace the military government that will have to be in power in this phase of transition, the Movement of the Armed Forces calls for calm and patriotism from all Portuguese and expects the country to support the powers instituted for its benefit.

"In this way we know we will have honoured the past in respect of policies assumed before the nation and others, and we are fully conscious of having complied with the sacred duty of restoring to the nation its legitimate and legal powers."

At the conclusion of the broadcast, an ancient cannon exploded from the heights of the old village, causing Paco and Cãozinho to race down the beach in search of safety. Paulo yelled at them to come back.

He ran to the square to hide himself in Amadeu's

and found it crowded with villagers, men and women, cheering the radio broadcast and drinking from bottles taken from behind the bar and passed around with only minimal protest from Amadeu himself.

"Viva Portugal!" was the predominant cry. "Viva la liberdade!"

The celebration continued throughout the day, with music and dancing and everyone drinking to excess. A group of fishermen went to the police station and escorted da Sousa to the square, where he was hanged from a fig tree, too low to kill him, that was not their intention, just to humiliate and cause discomfort around the neck. In a disoriented state, fearful of torture, but more of embarrassment, he confessed to his crime.

"Either shoot me or throw me in jail, but please, don't leave me here to shit myself like an idiot. It was an accident. She was crying and I accidentally suffocated her."

No one paid any attention to the whimpering from the fig tree, and in their excitement they simply forgot about him.

Paulo went to see Margaret Brown at her apartment, and finding her gone drove to the Quinta dos Angelicus to tell her the excellent news and perform his duties.

She hobbled towards him with the aid of her walking stick.

"I have already fed them, Paulo. You may go home."

Paulo did not quite understand, and with exasperated theatrics, Margaret Brown mimed the actions of feeding, pointed at herself, and shooed him away with her stick.

"My job!"

"Not any longer," she replied. "I agreed to your deal, and I do not want you interfering. You may wait until I'm in the ground, and, God help me, I'll be buried here to haunt you for the rest of your life."

Paulo walked to the kennel and opened the door. A short blow on his flute and the dogs grew excited. They ran out of the kennel, and in the ensuing mêlée the pair of Great Danes playfully jumped on Margaret Brown and sent her sprawling against the ground. She wailed on impact and knew that her hip was broken. When she called Paulo's name, he ignored her, got into Luís's van and turned on the loudspeaker. He used the microphone to broadcast his flute and in this fashion led the entire collection of dogs back into the village.

THIRTY-THREE

A Revolution of Carnations

 AS THEY TRIED TO FLUSH out pockets of resistance, troops chased fugitive secret policemen from house to house near the security headquarters. An angry crowd had gathered outside the building, shouting abuse at the police and watching for any attempting to escape. Some policemen slipped out of the building and through a cordon of troops to seek refuge in the maze of alleyways nearby. A number of civilians joined in the chase and a few soldiers fired at rooftops where the suspected fugitives hid from the wrath of the crowd.

"The junta cannot in any way accept the creation of a climate of irresponsibility," said General Spínola at a press conference from the tank-ringed headquarters of the Armed Forces Movement at the National Assembly building. "It would be extremely painful for the junta to have to adopt measures to repress excesses. I urge the media to ask the country to avoid extreme attitudes."

Extreme attitudes prevailed. As Luís and Luisa tried to make their way to inquire at the security headquarters, they were forced to stop by an angry man urging on a group that had cornered a former secret policeman, chased through six blocks of hilly streets and into a house with a heavy door.

"The man inside is a member of the political police who informed on students at the university," he shouted. "He has killed a thousand men. We'll hang him from the Salazar bridge. We'll hang them all and let their bodies rot, their skeletons to become a permanent monument to the revolution."

The spectators cheered.

Military policemen, red carnations pinned to their berets, arrived and calmly pushed the crowd back from the door. One of them rang the doorbell, waited, then banged on the door with his rifle butt. There was no answer, so two husky youths pushed through the crowd and banged their shoulders against the door, but it did not give. A corporal shoved a magazine into his automatic rifle and released the safety catch, but he kept the weapon pointed into the air, its butt resting on his hip.

"Move back, please," he said with a smile, and the pair shrugged and melted back into the crowd.

Luís, finally seeing an opportunity to participate, however insignificantly, climbed onto the hood of a car and yelled hoarsely: "The man inside is armed. We don't want anybody to be hurt. Keep back and let the army do its job. They have performed it well so far."

The crowd cheered Luís's words and were subdued, but only briefly.

A rock crashed through a window and a woman with a tense face poked her head out of one on the side of the building, peering out cautiously through the hanging wash.

A howl went up from the crowd and a soldier climbed on the back of a military vehicle and talked to her. Her brow furrowed several times as the soldier spoke to her.

"It's the killer's wife," yelled a woman. "He's in there. Let's get her too."

Munching their sandwiches, the soldiers again pushed the crowd back gently. A drunken sailor fell down and there was laughter as someone helped him to his feet.

Four soldiers moved in front of the locked door and pointed their weapons at it. The crowd became silent and the door cracked open. The worried woman's face appeared again and the soldiers formed a tight knot around the door. A shadowy figure appeared behind the woman as the door swung open.

His hands in the air, a man stepped forward to chants of "Killer! Killer!" and within seconds he was tumbled onto the floor of the military vehicle and the soldiers were on board.

"I don't wish to be a part of this, Luís," whispered Luisa. "It frightens me. Please. Why don't we take our honeymoon and we'll come back after to tell my father, once things have calmed down."

"But it is a great day in history. Do you really want to miss it?"

"It is a day in your history, but not really mine. My liberation was when I came to you. I'd prefer now to be on the road . . . and with you alone."

He stooped to pick up a trampled carnation, and placed it behind her ear.

"Thank you. Let's go, then."